Allen Coffin

The Coffin Family

The Life of Tristram Coffyn, of Nantucket, Mass. Founder of the Family

Line in America

Allen Coffin

The Coffin Family
The Life of Tristram Coffyn, of Nantucket, Mass. Founder of the Family Line in America

ISBN/EAN: 9783337414986

Printed in Europe, USA, Canada, Australia, Japan

Cover: Foto ©Raphael Reischuk / pixelio.de

More available books at **www.hansebooks.com**

THE COFFIN FAMILY.

THE LIFE

OF

TRISTRAM COFFYN,

OF NANTUCKET, MASS.,

FOUNDER OF THE FAMILY LINE IN AMERICA;

TOGETHER WITH

REMINISCENCES AND ANECDOTES OF SOME OF HIS NUMER-
OUS DESCENDANTS, AND SOME HISTORICAL IN-
FORMATION CONCERNING THE ANCIENT
FAMILIES NAMED COFFYN.

BY ALLEN COFFIN, LL.B.

NANTUCKET:
PUBLISHED BY HUSSEY & ROBINSON.
1881.

Benefit of Memorial Fund.

The Grand Memorial Exercises, commemorating the anniversary of the death of Tristram Coffyn, which was observed with appropriate ceremonies at Nantucket, Mass., on the 16th, 17th and 18th days of August, 1881, having passed into history, and received most gratifying encomiums from the press of America, a growing interest in the family history is noted from the increased correspondence brought to the Secretary's table.

Souvenirs of the celebration are sought for by many who could not be present, and many who had not previously been apprised of the affair seek information concerning it. In answer to some of the inquiries, and in anticipation of others, the following statements are presented:

The tables at the banquet on the 18th were laid with China decorated with the Coffyn Coat of Arms, of two varying styles. Those desiring were permitted to purchase the plate and cup and saucer used on the occasion. Several persons have since ordered whole dinner and tea sets of the same decoration, which can be multiplied to any extent. Single pieces of the identical ware used at the banquet can be obtained of the Secretary at the same prices as sold from the tables. Plate, $1 ; cup and saucer, $1.

There were also offered for sale the following :

The Life of Tristram Coffyn, of Nantucket, founder of the family line in America; together with reminiscences and anecdotes of some of his numerous descendants, and some historical information concerning the ancient families named Coffyn. By Allen Coffin, LL.B., Secretary of the Tristram Coffin Reunion Association. Price in cloth, $1 ; paper covers, 62 cents. Sent by mail.

Fine large photographs of Tristram Coffin, in the costume of the cavalier of 1642, as he is represented upon the Admiral Sir Isaac Coffin medal, and presented to the Association by George H. Folger, Esq., of Boston. Price, $1.

Elegant large-sized pictures of the old Coffin mansion, built at Newbury in 1652, where Tristram Coffin is supposed to have resided before removing to Nantucket, taken by the Albertype process, and presented to the Association by William E. Coffin, Esq., of Boston, Mass. Price, $1.

Photographs of eight ancient oil portraits of different members of the Coffin family, of Portledge, in North Devon, England, the originals of which were mostly executed in the sixteenth century, are also for sale. The original English copies furnished by Mr. William Edward Coffin, of Richmond, Ind. Price for the set, $1.50.

Also, the Coffin Coat of Arms, printed from the identical copper-plate used by Capt. Hector Coffin in his lifetime, which is a fine specimen of copper-plate engraving, and answers in general description to the Coat of Arms granted Admiral Sir Isaac Coffin, Bart., in 1804. The copper-plate was kindly loaned by its owner, Mr. Charles H. Coffin, of New Bedford, Mass. Price, 15 cents.

Any of the above articles can be obtained by addressing

ALLEN COFFIN, Secretary and Treasurer,

NANTUCKET, MASS.

PREFACE.

In presenting to the public this brief outline of the history of the Coffin family, the author is not unmindful of its many imperfections. The work first undertaken was soon perceived would require years to perfect. A full and correct history and genealogy of the Coffin family cannot be compiled without immense labor, and would be of little value unless accurate in details.

Desirous of offering to the great gathering of the descendants of Tristram Coffyn, to assemble in August, 1881, some information respecting the origin, rise, and development of this numerous family, the author notwithstanding his fear of disappointing the reasonable expectations of fr... submitted this humble production, in the hope that it will receive... siderate judgment of its readers, and possibly aid the future histor... shall attempt a more comprehensive family history.

No statement of fact is made without citing its authority; and... the facts cited, the author has drawn conclusions at variance with... accepted opinions, he is persuaded that the facts amply warrant su... departure. While some historical facts are believed to be here coll... presented for the first time, the author by no means concludes tha' t of investigation is exhausted, or that further research may not sti essentially change results.

Mr. William E. Coffin, of Richmond, Ind., kindly placed value' le scripts from his own pen, and a large collection of other documen papers, in the author's hands, who here expresses a fervent gratitud for. John Coffin Jones Brown, Esq., of Boston, placed the auth' obligations for valuable assistance in searching the noble libraries of particularly in the domain of heraldry. And for other valuable sug and literary aid, the author is indebted to George Howland Folger, Cambridge, Mass., William C. Folger, Esq., Mr. Alfred Swain, an Stella L. Chase, of Nantucket. The entire proceeds of the sale will plied to the Memorial Fund.

THE COFFIN FAMILY.

TRISTRAM COFFYN, (as he always signed his name,) the founder of the family line in America, and from whom all persons by the name of Coffin in this country are descended, was born at Brixton, a small parish and village, near Plymouth, in the southwestern part of Devonshire County, England, in the year 1605. He married Dionis Stevens, daughter of Robert Stevens, esquire, of Brixton, and, in 1642, emigrated to America with his wife, five small children, his widowed mother, and two unmarried sisters. He lived alternately in Salisbury, Haverhill and Newbury, in the Colony of Massachusetts, until 1659, when he came to Nantucket, then under the jurisdiction of New York, and made arrangements for the purchase of the island by a company which he organized at Salisbury. He returned to the island with his family in 1660, where he lived until his death, which happened on the 2d day of October, A. D. 1681, at his new residence on the hill, at Northham, near Capaum Pond, at the age of 76 years.

Coffin is a word of Hebrew origin, signifying a small basket. Whether the Israelitish hosts were sufficiently enlightened to be in the enjoyment of baskets before the Egyptians, or whether the chosen people of God were especially favored with a knowledge of the art of basket-making while the rest of the world plodded on with less commodious means of transit, are matters which cannot at this remote period of time be satisfactorily answered. But when, according to sacred history, we read that a multitude, from a desert place, were fed with five loaves and two fishes, and there was taken up of the fragments that remained twelve ᵇᵃˢᵏᵉᵗˢ full, we may be assured that baskets flourished among the Jews ᵃⁿᵗᵉʳⁱᵒʳ to the Christian era; so, of course, small baskets, or coffins, are ᵒᶠ ʲᵉwish origin.

ᶠʳᵒᵐ Arthur's "Derivation of Family Names," we find that Coffin is ᵗʰᵉ ᵂᵉˡˢʰ Cyffin, which signifies a boundary, a limit, or a hill; Cefyn a ᵗᵒᵖ of a hill. This authority also says the name has its origin from ᶜᵒ high, exalted, and fin, a head, extremity, boundary, but the family

surname is probably not indebted to either of these last-named deriva-
tions. It is believed by many that, some time before the Norman Conquest of England by William, which took place in 1066, the family of
Coffin lived in Normandy, a duchy of France, which the Norsemen had
made peculiarly their own by invasion and conquest. And it has been
claimed by some of the enthusiastic descendants of Tristram that the
Coffins, in the Old World, prevailed before the time of the Pharaohs, and
in the New World, came in with the Mayflower. Yet both of these statements are unfounded. The civilization of the East had doubtless pressed
westward as far as the English Channel before the Northern horses,
under that rude and impetuous Scandinavian chieftain, named Rollo, in-
vaded that portion of France which subsequently became Normandy.
And it is possible that the ancestors of the Coffin family passed from
Palestine to Greece several centuries before the Christian era, and, some
time later, from Greece to the southern part of France. If, however, a
trace from Palestine is admitted, it is none the less conclusive that the
valor and military prowess of the Norsemen became the controlling element in the Norman French character from the time of Rollo, A. D. 912,
up to the time of the Norman Conquest of England, when the name of
Coffyn first appears in English history. The distinguishing traits of the
Coffin family since it made a history are not Hebraic but either Norse or
ancient Briton.' I incline to the belief that our Norman ancestors came
down in early times with the vast military hordes which passed through
the German Ocean and the British seas, encountering every imaginable
peril, both by sea and land, and braving every hardship and privation of
fleet and camp, to find a region of country more congenial and pro-
ductive than their own native Scandinavia. They were the great navigators of their age. And their descendants, in our own time, from Nantucket as well as from other parts of New England, have shown the
same energy and endured like hardships in pursuing the whale-fishery in
the Pacific Ocean, and in sending whole fleets of adventurers more than
half way round the globe to dig for gold in California and Australia.
But this same hardy experience may have been gained from the life in
Devonshire, England, which developed some of the bravest navigators
and most daring spirits that ever upheld the English flag, like Sir Walter
Raleigh and Sir Francis Drake, who were born and reared in the south
part of Devonshire, whence Tristram Coffyn came.

What, in the Middle Ages, was called an invasion, we now term
expedition. Our historians are wont to designate these hardy self
liant adventurers which overran and conquered the countries lying
either side of the British Channel as barbarians; but I am persuaded
that in both instances—the Danes in England and the Swedes and Nor-
wegians in France—brought and maintained a higher type of civilizat-
in these respective countries than had hitherto existed there.

The Eastern civilization was met and absorbed by the Norse at the very time when personal individual names were becoming crystallized with second designations which we call surnames. The simple individual surnames we find in use throughout all pre-Norman history; but they seem to have been only for the life of him to whom they were attached, and died with him. It was not till the eleventh century that surnames can be said to have become hereditary, or in any true sense stationary; yet there were marked exceptions growing out of the peculiar conditions of feudal tenures in Normandy. The name of Coffin may belong to this exceptional class, which, commencing in France anterior to the Norman Conquest, in the pale mazes of uncertainty, has survived the mutations of eight centuries in England, to which it was first transplanted, and, from the American branch, in little more than two and one-half centuries, has become firmly engrafted upon the Western Continent, and returned many scions back unto the Old World from which they sprang.

Speaking of names derived from occupations, Bardsley, in his English Surnames, says: "It is to some dealer in earthenware we owe the name of 'Pots,' some worker in metals our 'Hammers,' some carpenter our 'Coffins,' once synonymous with 'Coffer.'" And he elsewhere says: "It is hard to say whether our 'Coffers' are relics of the old *Coffrer* or *Coifer*, but as the latter business was all but entirely in the hands of females, perhaps it will be safer to refer them to the other." Again he says: "Our 'Coffers,' relics of the old 'Ralph le Cofferer' or 'John le Cofferer,' though something occupative, were nevertheless official also, and are to be found as such in the thirteenth century. They remind us of the day when there were no such things as check-books, nor banks, nor a paper-money currency. Then, on every expedition, be it warlike or peaceful, solid gold or silver had to be borne for the baron's expenditure and that of his retinue; therefore none would be more important than he who superintended the transit from place to place of the chest of solid coinage, set under his immediate care." The cofferer was the treasurer of the royal or baronial retinue, and from the office was derived the name. And he further says: "Our 'Coffers' represent seemingly the same word in a two-fold capacity. We find occasional records where the cofferer was undoubtedly an official servant, a treasurer, one who carried the money of his lord in his journeyings up and down. More often, however, he was a tradesman, a maker or dealer in coffers or coffins, the two words being once used altogether indiscriminately." We may never feel satisfactorily assured that the name Coffin was both official and occupative; but that it was one or the other in its origin no doubt may longer exist. If you turn to the ancient version of the New Testament, in what is known as Wicklyffe's translation, and read the story of the five loaves and two fishes, in Mark vi, 43, you will find that the word coffyns is used in place of baskets, the verse reading thus: " And they token the relyves of broken mete, twelve coffyns full." Thus it will be seen that this word originated back, far back, in the gray morning twilight of Asiatic life, in the nomadic period of man's existence, before the Bethlehem shepherds guarded their flocks by night on Judea's plains. Moving westward with the march of empire it ret[a]ined its significance upon the borders of the English Channel, survivin[g] the destructiveness of the Norwegian adventurers of the ninth cen[tu]ry; and, becoming Normanized, it was first used as a sign-name, and then adopted as a surname from the official or business occupation, feudalism making it hereditary.

William the Conqueror, was born at Fallaise, a town of Normandy, France, in the department of Calvados, 22 miles S. S. E. of Caen, on the river Ante, in the year 1024. It is now a town of about 15,000 inhabitants, having still in the ruins of its ancient castle one of the finest towers in France. The town is built upon cliffs commanded by an old Norman castle and surrounded by a picturesque country. An equestrian bronze statue of William was erected here in 1851. Within two short leagues of Fallaise stands the old chateau of Courtiton, once the home of the Norman Coffins, the family name having now become extinct in that vicinage. The present owner, Mons. Le Clerc, is the grandson of the last Miss Coffin, the estate having descended in an unbroken male line, as is supposed, until her accession. She married, in 1796, from which time the name of Le Clere has succeeded to that of Coffin as possessors of this ancient estate. Admiral Henry E. Coffin, of the English Navy, a nephew of Admiral Sir Isaac, is the authority for the last statement. In a letter to Mr. William E. Coffin, of Richmond, Ind., written in October, 1880, he thus describes this old Norman chateau which he had several times visited: "It stands at the bottom of a hill in front of a lake. The drive to it is through ornamented wood, a zig-zag road descending to it. There is only the dining-room, kitchen, and part of the old house remaining, and the new part has two drawing-rooms built two hundred years ago, but looking nice."

It was upon this old estate, perhaps, that the first Norman Coffyn, of English fame, was born; and, being one of the younger sons, having no hope of an inheritance, if he rose to distinction in life it must be by his own endeavors. Reared within two leagues of Fallaise, he may have often sported with the youthful William, and been a favored guest at the Ducal Palace. When William's father, Robert, made his pilgrimage to the Holy Sepulchre, never to return, Coffyn's father may have share[d] in the vicissitudes of that expedition; and, if in the capacity of keep of the Duke's strong box, the name of Coffyn may have dated from th[e] return of that mournful retinue as an individualized surname.

From the time of the Norman Conquest the family of Coffin has been well known in England, according to Prince's Worthies of Devon, and there is some reason for supposing that members of this family came over before the Conquest and settled in Somerset and Devon and Dorset, for it is an undisputed fact that many Norman families took up their residences in England before the landing of William, and that some of them received favors from Edward the Confessor. When the Conqueror ordered the "Great Survey of all Lands," completed some twenty years after the battle of Hastings, the Coffins were entered in Domesday Book as being possessed of several hides land, as stated by Sir William Pole in his MSS. of "Devon and its Knights, in the reigns of the earlier Kings of England." A "hide land" was an uncertain quantity, supposed to be as much arable land as would maintain a family, and was a term used by the Saxons in measuring land, before the Norman French language was introduced as the regular language of the courts of law. In 1086, when Domesday was compiled, the conquered Saxons found that such of them as opposed the Conqueror in any manner had their lands confiscated. And the lands thus confiscated were granted out by the Conqueror to his faithful followers. Thus all the land in the kingdom " not possessed by the Church was held by the King in demesne, or of him directly, or of the honors he had seized and retained, as feuds, by comparatively few individuals." The lands granted were not given freely and without price, but were to be held of the King, subject to the performance of certain military duties as the condition of their enjoyment.

The most ancient seat of the name and family of Coffin in England, is now called Portledge, in the parish of Alwington, near Bideford, County of Devon. If it has been in the family from the settlement of the estates by Domesday, there can be little doubt that it was granted to Sir Richard Coffyn, Knight, for valuable services rendered the Conqueror, in that wonderfully romantic feudal age, when the barons and knights and esquires and serjeants became proprietors of vast estates, including castles, abbeys, villages, and even entire towns, throughout England. The great antiquity of the Coffins is further established, says Prince, by a boundary deed made near the time of the Conquest, and written in Saxon, between Richard Coffin, Lord of the Manor of Alwington and Cockementon, and the Abbot of Tavistock, in relation to the Abbey lands of Tavistock in the parish of Abbotsham near adjoining Alwington. One of the covenants was that "the Abbot and Convent of Tavistock should give to the said Richard Coffyn and his next heir, full fraternity in his Church of Tavistock, to receive there the habit of religion whenever (God so inspiring) they would; and that in the meantime they should have the privilege of one monk there."

Feudal tenures, or holding of the King, were introduced with other Norman customs and upheld and interpreted by the Norman lawyers,

who naturally adhered to the precedents they were used to in the   old
country.   Of the rule of primogeniture Maine's Ancient Law   say:
"The ideas and social forms which contributed to the formation of the
system were unquestionably barbarian and archaic; but as soon as
courts and lawyers were called in to interpret and define it, the princi-
ples of interpretation which they applied to it were those of the latest
Roman jurisprudence, and were, therefore, excessively refined and
matured. In a patriarchically governed society the eldest son may succeed to the government of the agnatic groupe and to the absolute disposal of its property. But he is not, therefore, a true proprietor. * *
* * *   The contact of the refined and barbarous nation had inevitably
for its effect, the conversion of the eldest son into legal proprietor of the
inheritance. The clerical and secular lawyers so defined his position
from the first; but it was only by insensible degrees that the younger
brother, from participating on equal terms in all the dangers and enjoy-
ments of his kinsman, sank into the priest, the soldier of fortune, or the
hanger-on of the mansion."

The family multiplied, and very early the younger sons of the first
Coffins domiciled in England, had established branches which appear to
have flourished in divers parts of Devonshire. The elder son always
succeeding to the estates until, from various causes, the feudal system of
tenures gradually gave way, and upon the restoration of Charles II. was
wholly abolished. Notwithstanding the feudal system of tenures in
England had long since passed into dissuetude, the form has, in some
instances, been preserved; and the Portledge manor, once including the
Parish of Alwington, is one of the very few estates in England which
have been held by the same family for six or seven centuries, the most
reliable historians of Devonshire all conceding that it has been in the
family for many centuries. I find the name of Coffin and Coffyn largely
identified with the County of Devon from its earliest reliable history.
Most writers upon the family name have considered Portledge, in the
northwestern part of the county, as the earliest home of the Coffins in
England, and, naturally enough, have come to the conclusion that Tristram Coffyn descended from that house. I have not, however, been
forced to any such conclusion. The present proprietor of Portledge,
John Richard Pine Coffin, a magistrate for Devon, and Lord of the
Manors of Alwington, Goldsworthy and Monkleigh, finds nothing in the
records of Portledge leading to such a conclusion. He does not even
find the family names of Tristram and Peter, and barely a Nicholas.
The earliest record of Portledge proprietors, as I infer from the list given
by the present proprietor, is that of Richard Coffin, A. D. 1254, a deed of
that date being a small charter of Henry III., in Latin, "whereby at the
instance of John de Courtenay, the sovereign grants to Ric. Coffin and
his heirs free warren in all his demesnes and lands of Alwington, in the

County of Devon." Another deed said to be the oldest among the family records of Portledge, in the same reign of Henry III., whereby Richard Cophin grants unto Thomas de Dudderigge certain lands.

Oliver's Ecclesiastical Antiquities of Devon (p. 24) mentions Nicholas Coffin, as vicar of the Church at Chudleigh, in the southeastern part of Devon, some 40 miles from Portledge, as early as 1357. Concerning this vicarage Rev. Mr. Oliver says: "The Church of Chudleigh forms the subject of a deed of John, Bishop of Exeter, between the years 1186 and 1191. The Parish Church was dedicated by Bishop Bronescombe, on the 6th of November, 1259." Among the incumbents, Nicholas (without a surname) is the first name met with. He is believed to be the vicar who bequeathed, in 1303, to the Fabric of Exeter Cathedral, vi s. viii d. John Fitz Hugh, occurs vicar the 29th of September, 1317. Nicholas Coffin, instituted the 20th of June, 1337. Thomas de Marston, the 23d of March, 1348. It is fair to presume that this Nicholas Coffin was vicar of the Chudleigh Church from the date of his institution, (1337) till the institution of his successor, in 1348.

The earliest mention of the name Coffin in any Heraldic Visitation of Devonshire is found in that of 1620, in connection with the family of le Moyne or Monk, the name changing from le Moyne to Monk about 1425. Hugh le Moyne, in the 3d year of the reign of Edward I., according to his pedigree, was descended from Peter le Moyne, who married Maude, daughter of Coffin of Beacombe. By allowing 30 years for a generation, Maude Coffin must have been born about 1140, and her father about 1110. It was from this family that the celebrated George Monk, Duke of Albemarle, was descended. He was conspicuous in the restoration of Charles II., the soldiers and populace poised upon his word, and when he declared for a free Parliament, their enthusiasm was unbounded. Of him Macauley says: "As soon as his declaration was known, the whole nation was wild with delight. Wherever he appeared thousands thronged round him shouting and blessing his name. The bells of England rang joyously; the gutters ran with ale; and night after night the sky five miles round London was reddened by innumerable bonfires."

The Coffin family has also been allied by intermarriages with many other honorable families, among them, may be found Chudleigh, Carey, Courtney, Beaumont, Prideaux, Clifford, and even with Royalty, having married granddaughters and great-granddaughters of William the Conqueror, Henry I. and Edward I.

Of Alphington Church, in the southeastern part of the county, near Exeter, (pp. 72-74,) Rev. Mr. Oliver says: "In front of the gallery is the date of its erection, 1632; and in the panels are several shields, some, I think, incorrectly blazoned. We observed Southcot's, Tothill's, Duck's, Oxenham's; Arms of the See of Exeter impaled with Dr. Hall's, then

Bishop of Exeter; Bourchier's, Earl of Bath, then the patron; Courtenay's impaled with Seymour's; Bampfylde's; Northleigh's; Coffin's, holders of property at Marsh Barton; Prust's, Holway's of Wadeton, Arms of the Taylor's Company, Exeter. * * * * * Within the parish was the ancient Cell or Priory, of St. Mary, dependant on Plympton Priory, and now commonly called Marsh Barton. * * * * * Soon after the dissolution of Religious Houses, Henry VIII. granted the scite with several messuages in Alphington, St. Thomas, and Newton St. Cyres parish, on Sept. 9, 1546, to James Coffin and Thomas Godwin. This James Coffin, on 10 Dec., 1562, sold to John Hoker, the historian, for £27, all the oak, ash, elm, and other trees standing in the grove, on the south part of the Mansion House of Marsh, between the running water on the S. and the open pasture adjoining the said Mansion on the N., and the great pool on the W., and a ditch on the E., together with some other oaks towards the S. E. part of the Mansion. Hardly a vestige of this Priory has been suffered to remain."

The parish of Coffin's Well, also in the southeastern part of Devon, has a chapel which is a dependant of St. Mary's Church. Domesday proves that St. Mary's Church, in the reign of Edward the Confessor, belonged to the Cathedral of Exeter. In St. Mary's Church is an epitaph of Margaret, the wife of John Holbrine, esquire, and daughter of William Fowlett, who died at Coffin's Well, 11th of May, 1526. In making note of this family, Mr. Oliver queries "Did they reside at the Barton near Coffin's Well Church?" The chapel at Coffin's Well he describes as "low, and measures with its tower (which contains four bells three of which are ancient) 72½ feet in length and 26 in breadth. A north aisle is united to the Chancel and Nave by four arches; on the south of the Chancel is a small Chantry 10 feet by 9. In a window of the north aisle I observed a figure of the Blessed Virgin with a label *Ave Maria, plena gracia*, as also a fragment of the sacred name I H S. The parochial registers begin with Christmas, 1560." In a note Mr. Oliver observes "This hamlet was originally called Welles. Several families, the Huretons, the Ferrers, the Foliots, held property here, which at last came to the Coffins. In fol. 47 of the Cartulary of Tor Abbey (now in Trinity College, Dublin) is an agreement between Simon, Abbot of Tor, and Robert Coffyn, in relation to certain tenements in Welles Coffyn, and release confirmatory thereof."

Westcote's Devonshire (p. 440) says: "There is Coffin's Well, belonging to the Coffin family. Of this family we find Sir Hugo Coffin, of Combe-Coffin, or Coffin-Pyne, in the age of Richard I. (1189–1199); Sir Hugh, of the same, in the time of Henry III. (1216–1272); and Sir Elias, of this place (Coffin's Well); but presently after, in Edward's reign, Sir Robert de Scobbahull; in later times, by the heir of Coll, it descended to Prideaux."

A recent writer in the Cornhill Magazine, under the title of Lyme Regis, describing the red coast of Devonshire, England, makes this mention of Combe-Pyne, formerly Combe-Coffin :

"From Beer and Seaton we may return to Lyme by the high road over Axbridge and close to Combe-Pyne—the first half of which is our old friend *combe*, a valley, while the second half belongs to the ancient lords of the manor, the famous Devonshire family of the Pynes. At a still earlier date Combe was the property of the Coffins, another great Devonshire house, and then bore the name of Combe-Coffin. Later on, the two families coalesced, and so gave origin to the ludicrous modern surname of Pyne-Coffin, borne by the branch of the old stock now settled at the Alwington House near Clovelly. Combe-Pyne, as its name suggests, is a pleasant little vale, where a tributary of the Axe has cut through the layer of chalk and reached the greensand below."

Combe-Pyne is in the extreme eastern part of Devon, bordering upon Dorset, and is allowed by Rev. Mr. Oliver to have once belonged to the Pyne family, and much more anciently to the family of Coffin. Henry de Medecroft de Wyke Risingdon being admitted to this Rectory of Comb-Coff, n. April 20, 1334.

Combe-Raleigh was occasionally called Combe-Coffin, as stated in a note, probably for the same reason that it also once belonged to the Coffin family.

From the post-office directory of Devonshire of recent issue a post office is noted at the parish of Spreyton, in the central part of the County called "Coffins."

Rev. Mr. Prince, in his Worthies of Devonshire, makes mention of "Coffin's Ingarly," [now probably Inwardleigh,] in the west part of the Province ; in which last place the Mansion House was near the Church, to which was belonging a fair deer park now wholly demolished.

In Hutching's History of Dorset (vol. i, p. 468) is the following account of the parish of Wambrook : "This little village, now a distinct parish, was anciently part of Chadstock, from which it lies about two miles north, on the very borders of the county, adjoining Somersetshire. A family of the Perceys were its lords. It afterwards came to the Filiols, of Woodlands, who held it from the 3d year of the reign of Henry V. to the 19th year of Henry VIII. In the 22d of Henry VIII., on the partition of Sir William Filiol's property, this manor was assigned to Sir Edward Kymer ; after this it passed to several private persons or owners. In 1645, Mr. Humphrey Coffin, recusant, had his old rents here, and his lands, valued in 1641, at £30 per annum, sequestered. In 1645, Mr. John Coffin's term here, valued at £45 per annum was sequestered."

In the war between Charles I. and the Parliament, Dorsetshire sided with the King, but was too weak to afford effectual aid. Our great ancestor, Tristram Coffyn, also held estates in Dorsetshire which were sequestered, during that same period of uncertain tenures in England

Of the parish of Alwington and the manor of Alwington, of Alwington House, and Portledge, a great deal has been written concerning, and much confusion arisen as to the real character of these places. It is proper to state that Portledge is a seat in the parish of Alwington, near the borough of Bideford, in North Devon, bordering upon Barnstaple Bay. Alwington parish, in 1876, had a population of 353; Bideford, a population of 6,969. Bideford is the great business centre of that locality, once a seaport of some consequence, and the post town, Portledge, lying only four miles away in a westerly direction. Charles Kingsley, in his "Westward Ho!" a romance of the "Voyages and Adventures of Sir Amyas Leigh, Knight of Burrough, in the County of Devon, in the reign of Queen Elizabeth," with graphic power of description, thus writes of this ancient borough: "All who have travelled through the delicious scenery of North Devon must needs know the little white town of Bideford, which slopes upward from its broad tide-river paved with yellow sands and many-arched old bridge where salmon wait for autumn floods, toward the pleasant upland on the west. Above the town the hills close in, cushioned with deep oak woods, through which juts here and there a crag of fern-fringed slate; below they lower, and open more and more in softly-rounded knolls, and fertile squares of red and green, till they sink into the wide expanse of hazy flats, rich salt marshes, and rolling sand-hills, where Torridge joins her sister Taw, and both together flow quietly toward the broad surges of the bar, and the everlasting thunder of the long Atlantic swell. Pleasantly the old town stands there, beneath its soft Italian sky, fanned day and night by the fresh ocean breeze, which forbids alike the keen winter frosts, and the fierce thunder heats of midland; and pleasantly it has stood there for now, perhaps, 800 years, since the first Grenville, cousin of the Conqueror, returning from the conquest of South Wales, drew round him trusty Saxon serfs, and free Norse rovers with their golden curls, and dark Silurian Britons from the Swansea shore, and all the mingled blood which still gives to the seaward folk of the next county their strength and intellect, and, even in these levelling days, their peculiar beauty of face and form."

In this pleasing romance, Mr. Kingsley has made prominent among its characters the name of Coffin, as one identified with the gentle folk of North Devon. Portledge is spoken of as the place where lived that most protestant justice of the peace, Mr. Coffin; and as the place where the Coffins had lived ever since Noah's flood. It appears that no one, whether writing of fact or fiction, discourses long about Devonshire without mentioning the family of Coffin, so thoroughly interwoven is it with the ancient history of Devon.

Some of these families in ancient times furnished gentlemen with gilded spurs, as well as names to localities. Prince mentions Sir Geoffrey

Coffin, of Combe-Coffin, in the days of King Henry III.; and, before that, Sir Elias Coffin, of Ingarly, (also called Sir Elias Coffin of Argot,) in the days of King John of England. Of the family at Alwington, from the time of Henry I. unto the age of Edward II., the period of more than 200 years, the heirs, it is claimed, were always called Richard; and we note Sir Richard Coffin, of Alwington, Knight, in the reign of Henry II.; Sir Richard Coffin, of Alwington, in the reign of Edward I.; and Sir Richard Coffin, in the days of Henry IV.; and again, a century afterward, Richard Coffin was high sheriff of Devon, in the second year of Henry VIII. Perhaps the most eminently distinguished of the family name in England at any period was Sir William Coffin, Knight, in the reign of King Henry VIII. He was born at Portledge, and was a younger brother of the Richard Coffin, who was high sheriff of Devon in the second year of Henry VIII., above mentioned. He married Lady Manors, of Darbyshire, and probably resided with her in Darbyshire, as he was chosen knight of that shire in the Parliament which began in the 21st year of the reign of Henry VIII. (1529). Though his elder brother, Richard, succeeded to the Portledge estate, Sir William became possessed of the manor of East Higginton, in the parish of Berrynarbor, in North Devon, some fifteen miles in a northerly direction from Portledge, and perhaps other estates in Devon, all of which, upon his death, dying without issue, he conveyed to his nephew, his eldest brother's son, Richard Coffin, of Portledge. Sir William's reputation was not confined to Devonshire. His education and accomplishments were such that they introduced him with advantage to the Court of Henry VIII., where he came to be highly preferred, and accompanied the King as one of the eighteen chosen to assist at the tournament held between him and the French King before Guisness, in France, A. D. 1519. This fact shows that he was a gentleman of courage and expert at feats of arms.

Of these jousts Camden says,—"They were at first public exercises of arms practised by noblemen and gentlemen, but soon became more than mere sports and diversions. They were first introduced A. D. 934, and were always managed by their own particular laws. A long time and in all parts their practise was continued, to that degree of madness and with so great a slaughter of persons of the best quality, especially here in England where it was more prominently introduced by Stephen, that the Church was forced by seven canons to forbid them with the penalty, 'that whosoever should happen therein to be slain should be denied Christian burial,' and under King Henry III. by the advice of Parliament it was enacted that the offenders' estate should be forfeited and their children disinherited, yet in contempt of that good law this evil and pernicious practise long prevailed."

Polwhele's Devonshire states that Sir William Coffin was Master of the Horse at the Coronation of Anne Boleyn, in the 25th year of Henry

VIII. (1534) ; and was afterward honored with knighthood in the 29th year of the same reign. He was also one of the gentlemen of the Privy Chamber to the same King, a place of great reputation and trust, whose office is to wait on the king within doors and without, so long as his majesty is on foot, and when the king eats in his Privy Chamber, they wait at table and bring in the meat ; they wait also at the reception of ambassadors, and every night two of them lie in the King's Privy Chamber. They are forty-eight in number, all knights or esquires of note, whose power is great ; for a gentleman of the Privy Chamber, by the King's command, only, without any written commission, is sufficient to arrest a Peer of England. These gentlemen were not at this time chosen to fill this office because of their political training and abilities alone, but because of their fine physical development and noble carriage and expertness in arms.

Another incident in the life of Sir William is related both by Mr. Prince and Mr. Polwhele, because it led to an act of Parliament which limited the power of priests in demanding mortuaries, and gave occasion for the confirmation of the observation "that evil manners are often the parent of good laws." On his way to the Parliament, in 1522, from Darbyshire, "Passing by a Church-yard, he saw a multitude of people standing idle ; he inquired into the cause thereof: they replied that they had brought a corpse thither to be buried, but the priest refused to do his office, unless they first delivered him the poor man's cow, the only quick goods he left for a mortuary. Sir William sent for the priest, and required him to do his office to the dead. He peremptorily refused unless he had his mortuary first. Whereupon he caused the priest to be put into the poor man's grave, and earth to be thrown in upon him, and as he still persisted in his refusal, there was still more earth thrown in, until the obstinate priest was either altogether, or well nigh suffocated.

"Now thus to handle a priest in those days, was a very bold adventure ; but Sir William Coffin, with the favor he had at Court, and the interest he had in the House, diverted the storm ; and so lively represented the mischievous consequences of priests arbitrarily demanding of mortuaries, that the then Parliament, taking it into their serious consideration, were pleased to bound that matter ever after, by a particular statute ; the preamble whereof, which runs thus, seems to intimate as much : 'Forasmuch as question, ambiguity, and doubt, is chanced and risen, upon the order, manner, and form of demanding, receiving, and claiming of mortuaries, otherwise called corps-presents, as well for the greatness and value of the same, which, as hath lately been taken, is thought over excessive to the poor people, and others of this realm, as also for that, &c.: Be it therefore enacted, &c.: First—That no mortuary shall be taken of any moveable goods, under the value of ten marks. Secondly—That no parson, &c., shall take of any person that, dying, &c., in moveable goods, clearly above his debts paid, above ten marks and under thirty pounds, above three shillings and four pence for a mortuary, in the whole. And for a person dying, or dead, having at the time of his death, of the value in moveable goods, of thirty pounds or above, clearly above his debts, and under the value of forty pounds, no more shall be taken for a mortuary than six shillings and eight pence, in the whole. And for any person having at the time of his death, of the value, in moveable goods, of forty pounds or above, to any sum whatsoever it be, clearly above his debts paid, there shall be no more taken, paid, or demanded, for a mortuary, than ten shillings in the whole.'

"What herein is further observable, it was also enacted, that such mortuaries shall be paid, only in such a place where heretofore mortuaries have been used to be paid; and that those mortuaries be paid only in the place of the deceased person's most usual habitation; and that no parson, &c., shall take more than as limited in this Act, under penalty of forfeiting every time so much in value, as they shall take above the sum limited by this Act, &c. So much for the occasion of this statute; which confirms the observation, that evil manners are often the parent of good laws."

Sir William was also high steward of the manor and liberties of Standon, in the county of Hereford, where he resided at the time of his death. He bequeathed to his great Master, King Henry VIII., with whom he had lived in intimate relations and especial grace and favor, his best horses and a cast of his best hawks. He was buried at Standon, in the parish church, under a flat stone, on which was some time found this inscription, as mentioned in Weever's Funeral Monuments, (p. 534):

"Here lieth William Coffin, Knight, sometime of the Privy Chamber with his Sovereign Lord, King Henry VIII.; and Master of the Horse unto Queen Anne, the most lawful Wife unto the aforesaid King Henry VIII. and High Steward of all the Liberty and Manor of Standon, in the county of Hereford, which William deceased the 8th day of December, in the Year of our Lord, 1538, the 30th of the reign of King Henry VIII."

The most that has hitherto been written in America upon the Coffin family of England, has been based upon the assumption that all of that name in England descended from ancestors of the Portledge family, and, consequently, that the American Coffins were also descendants from Portledge. There is not, however, the slightest evidence that Portledge is the most ancient seat of the Coffins in England. That it has descended in a direct line from a very great antiquity, is true; that it has been the abode of gentlemen of culture and learning is notorious; for Mr. Prince tells us that the Richard Coffin who possessed the estate at the time of his writing was a "right worthy and worshipful gentleman of great piety and virtue," that he was especially learned in venerable antiquity, and had a noble library which he knew well how to make use of. And in every article upon the Coffins that has fallen under my eye pertaining to the antiquity of the family, notwithstanding some of them claim to have been copies from ancient manuscripts, there are unmistakable marks of having been made up from Mr. Prince's history of the Worthies of Devon.

The Rev. John Prince wrote his work as other works of that kind were written, from material at hand, about A. D. 1690. He refers to Sir William Pole's MSS., from which he quotes. He had doubtless examined the MSS. of Portledge, and gathered information from the proprietor, who was also a gentleman of literary and antiquarian tastes. He makes the Portledge family prominent, and, at the time of his writing, it was probably the most important family of the name of Coffin in Devonshire, as it now is. He says he finds a Sir Richard Coffin, of Alwington, Knight, as far back as the days of King Henry II., and that the manor of Alwington hath been in the name of Coffin from the time of the Norman Conquest unto this day; but he gives us no evidence of that fact by citing any deed or document. And, in a recent publication called "The MSS. of J. R. P. Coffin, Esq., at Portledge, N. D.," to which the compiler's name is not appended, although he was the guest of the proprietor, no such pretention is made. The earliest date to any deed is that of 1254. This writer did not find the Saxon deed mentioned by Prince as having been made near the Conquest, although an interpretation of it is given. Westcote's Devonshire (p. 314) says "Allington, Alwington, Alwinton, and, in Domesday Book, Hanitine, for by all these names it is written, was possessed by David de la Bear." "Portledge therein was held by one of the name, by the heir of which race it came to the ancient and dignous family of Coffin, which in former times were of great estate, for in the time of Richard I. (1189–1199) I find Sir Hugo Coffin of Combe Coffin; in Henry III. (1216–1272) Sir Geoffrey Coffin of the same place."

Now, if Alwington was recorded in Domesday as the property of David de la Bear, and Portledge held by one of that name, by the heir of which it subsequently passed into the family of Coffin, the claim that this estate has been possessed by the family of Coffin from the Conquest must fail. The Sir Hugo Coffin and Sir Geoffrey Coffin had nothing to do with Portledge. It is as probable that the Coffins who first held Portledge descended from the Coffins of Combe Coffin, as otherwise; and yet, the earliest family of Coffins may have come over with the Conqueror, or before that time, as previously stated.

Brixton, where Tristram Coffyn held estates, lies near the southern coast of Devonshire, some forty miles away from Portledge, which lies on the northwestern coast; and there is no evidence that the Portledge Coffins ever held property in Brixton. Combe Coffin lies sixty miles away on the southeastern coast near Dorsetshire. Coffins Well is about fifty miles distant, also on the southeastern coast. Chudleigh, where

Nicholas Collin was vicar of the Church in 1337, lies forty miles away. These distances are insignificant now, but, with the means of transit in the time of the first William, and all the later kings down to the introduction of steam, they are quite significant.

Polwhele (VI, p. 197) says: "From the time of Vortigern to the Norman Conquest and from the Conquest to Edward the First, (1272–1307) we have little to contemplate in the civil and military transactions of Devonshire, but revolution, massacre, and disorder." And, from the time of Edward I. to Charles I., it cannot be said that England enjoyed any long period of domestic tranquility, and Devonshire was subject to many turmoils and convulsions. It was upon the southern coast of Devonshire that the principal conflicts were waged. It was from this part of the country that such men as Sir Francis Drake and Sir Walter Raleigh were reared. Portledge stood to the north away from the scenes of revolution and pillage, and the fact that its tenures have not been disturbed for six centuries or more, and its records preserved through so long a period of time, is sufficient for the inferential conclusion that its favored locality alone saved it to the family, through all the vicissitudes of the frequently recurring insurrections and invasions that menaced and devastated the southern parts of Devon.

The civil wars between the houses of York and Lancaster, which for more than half a century, commencing in the reign of Henry VI., deluged England in blood, wrought great changes in the estates of Devonshire. And again, during the religious throes which characterized the several reigns from Henry VIII. to Charles I., the dissolution of religious houses, and the spoliation of Abbey lands; together with the restoration of the old order of things under the Catholics, all wrought disorder in Devonshire; and, while some of the Coffins—notably those from Portledge—realized great advantages in the time of Henry VIII., it is probable that others suffered persecution and perhaps martyrdom.

While many have searched for the pedigree of our ancestor, Tristram Coffyn, among the records of Devonshire, no one has yet been able to trace his pedigree beyond that of his grandfather, Nicholas Coffyn. Admiral Sir Isaac Coffin, Bart., in memorializing the College of Arms, in 1804, for the grant of a Coat of Arms, represented that he was by tradition descended from the family of Coffin of the west of England, but that he was unable to ascertain his descent. I have faith, however, that the proper investigation of the matter will sometime reveal to us Tristram's true pedigree extending much further back; and that what is now unknown will prove as honorable as that which we now know with reasonable certainty.

Tristram Coffyn, of Butler's, parish of Brixton, county of Devon, England, made his will November 16, 1601, which was proved at Totness, in the same county, in 1602. He left legacies to Joan, Anne, and

A1

John, children of Nicholas Coffyn; Richard and Joan, children of Lionel Coffyn; Philip Coffyn and his son Tristram; and appointed Nicholas, son of Nicholas Coffyn, his executor. He was probably the great uncle of the first of the race in America.

Nicholas Coffyn, of Brixton (one account says Butler's Parish), in Devonshire, in his will, dated September 12, 1613, and proved November 3, 1613, mentions his wife, Joan, and sons Peter, Nicholas, Tristram, John, and daughter Anne. He was the grandfather of the emigrant to New England.

Peter Coffyn, of Brixton, in his will, dated December 1, 1627, and proved March 13, 1628, provides that his wife, Joan (Thember) shall have possession of the land during her life, and then the said property shall go to his son and heir, Tristram, "who is to be provided for according to his degree and calling." His son John is to have certain property when he becomes 20 years of age. He mentions his daughters Joan, Deborah, Eunice and Mary, and refers to his tenement in Butler's Parish called Silferhay. He was the father of the emigrant.

John Coffyn, of Brixton, an uncle of the emigrant, who died without issue, in his will, dated January 4, 1628, and proved April 3, 1628, appoints his nephew, Tristram Coffyn, his executor, and gives legacies to all of Tristram's sisters, all under 12 years of age.

Nicholas Coffyn, the grandfather of Tristram, was probably born about the middle of the sixteenth century, in the reign of Edward VI. (1550). He lived to the end of the reign of the Tudors, and saw the reign of the Stuarts commenced in the person of James VI. of Scotland and I. of England. He died in the reign of James I. (1613). His eldest son, Peter, doubtless succeeded to his estates; and his youngest son, John, acquired some estate, as he made our Tristram his executor. The other sons, Nicholas and Tristram, have not been accounted for, neither has his daughter Anne.

Peter Coffyn, the father of Tristram, must have been born during the reign of Queen Elizabeth, about the year 1580. He died about the close of the year 1627 or early in the year 1628. At present we know of but little more of Tristram's father than we do of his grandfather, save that he married Joan Thember (or Thumber) and had two sons and four daughters, of whom Tristram was the eldest, the other son, John, having died in Plymouth Fort, England, after receiving a mortal wound.

Tristram Coffyn was born at Brixton, near Plymouth, county of Devon, England, during the reign of James I., in the year 1605, as previously stated. He married Dionis Stevens, daughter of Robert Stevens, Esq., of Brixton, about the year 1630. The particular causes or circumstances which induced his emigration to America have been a subject of profound study and mature deliberation. If we look at the contemporaneous history of England we shall find that the time which covers Tristram's mature life in England, about fifteen years, marks a most eventful period—the moment when intellectual freedom was claimed unconditionally by Englishmen as an inalienable right, and when ecclesiastical forms were not spared by the revolutions of the time.

James I., whose reign had been adorned by Shakespeare and Bacon, died in 1625, when Tristram was 20 years old. Charles I. had been upon the Throne but two years when Tristram's father died. The Petition of Right, in 1628, sought to limit the powers of the Crown, and the King soon after abolished the Parliament and established the Star Chamber. Puritanism was making rapid strides, and large numbers of Puritans were leaving England. So great was the exodus that the King prohibited their departure, and Hampden, Pym, and Cromwell were prevented from leaving. About this time the Duke of Buckingham was assassinated. In 1638 the Scotts, to maintain their ecclesiastical rights, took up arms against the King, having framed the celebrated Solemn League and Covenant, and sustained the Parliament in its opposition to Charles. The Earl of Strafford and the Archbishop of Canterbury, as chief advisers of the King, were impeached and beheaded (the former in 1641, and the latter in 1644). The Presbyterians, who were now a majority in the Commons, procured the exclusion of the Bishops from the House of Lords, in 1641, which was followed by an act, in 1643, entirely abolishing the Episcopacy, so that Charles began to realize that without Bishops there would be no King. Under these circumstances the Long Parliament convened.

The irrepressible conflict between Charles I. and the Parliament came to a crisis in 1642, and in August of that year the royal standard was raised at Nottingham. The King was generally supported by the nobility, the landed gentry, the High Church party, and the Catholics; and the Parliament was sustained by the mercantile and middle classes and the lower order of the great towns.

Tristram Coffyn was of the landed gentry. Most probably he was a Churchman after the order of Elizabeth's time. Conformably to his father's will he was to be provided for "according to his degree and calling." He must, therefore, have had a calling—a profession. He may have taken holy orders or practiced at Exeter *nisi prius*, (although there appears but little in his life at Nantucket to warrant the belief that he ever pretended to anything more than plain Mister Tristram Coffyn). Yet it does appear that the very year of the appeal to arms, 1642, after the conflict had been waged, Tristram Coffyn, at the age of 37, left all of his comfortable estates in Old England and embarked for America, bringing with him his wife and five small children, his mother, then aged 58 years, and two unmarried sisters, and none of them ever returned.

The question will occur again and again to the minds of the thoughtful, Why did Tristram Coffyn leave England at this particular time, and in what ship did he embark? Upon these subjects he has left no record and the oracles are silent. It is difficult to conceive how a man of his positive character could have lived in South Devon, during the stormy times of Charles I., and not have taken some part in the fierce conflicts which ensued. He must have had convictions, and he probably did not conceal them. If he was of the Parliament party it would be hard to divine the motive that prompted his emigration just at the time when that party was successful and gaining strength and power. And if of the King's party, why he should have abandoned a failing cause, with his tenacity of opinion. There are several versions of the cause of his emigration. One is to the effect that *Colonel* Tristram Coffyn was Governor of Plymouth, and in command of Plymouth Fort, after it fell into the possession of the Parliament party; and, upon the restoration of Charles II., expecting nothing but persecution from that monarch, he resigned command of the Citadel and embarked for America. This statement cannot be true in any particular, because he arrived in America in 1642, and Charles II. did not return to England till 1660. Another version is that, being Governor of Plymouth, and in command of the Fort, upon finding he could not longer hold the Citadel against the Parliament forces, prepared a vessel and embarked for America with his family. This last statement although more probable, is equally unfounded in fact; for there would have remained some history of the fact if he had ever been Governor of Plymouth, or commanded the Fort.

It must be borne in mind that Plymouth fell into the power of the Parliament at the very commencement of the civil war, and, though long besieged and blockaded by the King's forces, was never reduced to his control. It must also be remembered that Tristram's only brother, John Coffyn, was mortally wounded at Plymouth Fort, and died eight days thereafter. Upon which side John Coffyn was enlisted we have no certain evidence, and the exact date of his death is not known. I assume that, being a younger son, he entered the military service of his country and accepted duty at Plymouth Fort, under Charles I. In what capacity it is not material, but most probably in a subordinate one; for, if he had been Governor of Plymouth, or in command of the Fort, that fact would have survived the historic demolition of that eventful period. John Coffyn most likely fell in defense of the royal standard, and, if so, he died at the commencement of the civil war.

Tristram Coffyn, as heir of his father's estates at Brixton, within about five miles of Plymouth, found himself established among the landed gentry, whose interests and sympathies were generally with the royal party. I assume, therefore, that Tristram was a royalist, without dissimulation. The family characteristics could no more be disguised in him in England than in Nantucket. He stood for what he was; and, when Plymouth, in 1642, fell under the control of the Parliament party, to stand for the royal cause at Brixton, almost within range of the cannon at Plymouth Fort, required courage, particularly after his only brother had fallen in defense of that cause. Yet he stood faithful to his convictions of right and loyal to the King. He was at this time in the prime of early manhood, just the proper age to have become enamored of the knightly bearings of the Cavaliers. But, while he adhered to the royal cause with fidelity and zeal, and was unquestionably a Cavalier, in contradistinction from the Roundheads, I cannot conclude, estimating him by his life in Nantucket, that he ever took any delight in horse soldiers or their decorations, although every inch a knight in the truest and most chivalric sense.

Considering the eventful period of his life immediately following the death of his father, which probably occurred early in 1628, when he had but attained his twenty-third year, it is easy to perceive how the perplexing complications of the King and the Parliament, gave him little peace of mind or enjoyment of his estate. The whole kingdom, in 1642, exhibited a most melancholy spectacle. Each county, town, and hamlet, was divided into factions seeking the ruin of each other. The two great armies plundered wherever they came, and their example was faithfully copied by smaller bodies of armed men. Every person was compelled to contribute after a certain rate to the support of that cause which obtained the superiority in his neighborhood. While the royalists triumphed in the northern counties, on the southern coast the superiority of the Parliament party was equally decisive.

It will be asked How could Tristram Coffyn, a royalist, leave Brixton, at a time when Plymouth and the whole southern coast was controlled by Parliament forces? And, if there had not been a pacific feeling among neighbors and an interruption of hostilities in Devon at this time, it could not have happened. But Lingard, in his History of England (v. 10, p. 120), states that there were four counties, "those of York, Chester, Devon, and Cornwall, in which the leaders had already learned to abhor the evils of civil dissention. They met on both sides and entered into engagements to suspend their political animosities, to aid each other in putting down the disturbers of the public peace, and to oppose the introduction of any armed force, without the joint consent of both the King and the Parliament." This period of pacific intercourse which subsequently became associated in other counties, took place in Devon, in 1642; and, under its operation, emigration to America offered a proper solution of the problems that had perplexed the mature life of Tristram Coffyn in England. What to him were lands and tenements, rents and revenues,—under the tyranny of a King which in levying ship-money made all estates insecure, or under the sway of a Parliament

which exacted a contribution of one-twentieth part of the estate for the
support of an army, where human life was always insecure, no matter
which party succeeded,—to the unconditional liberty of body and soul
which the wilderness of America offered. Saddened by the early decease
of an only brother in a cause, whic.. f successful, offered nothing but
oppression; sickened ... . ontiona' revolution and anarchy which
surrounded ... early sone, acquietly quitted his otherwise ample and
comfortable estates in the Old World, and sought a home midst the hardy
Pilgrim settlers of the New. It was h. utter want of faith in the insti-
tutions of England that sent ... across the ocean with a wife and five
small children, a widowed mother and two unmarried dependant sisters,
to found a new home among the barren hills of New England. While
he could not bring his landed estates, he doubtless did not come penni-
less.

Admiral Henry E. Coffin, R. N., in his correspondence with Mr.
William E. Coffin, of Richmond, Ind., states that Tristram Coffyn's estate
at Brixton, upon the Restoration, was given by Charles II. to his bastard
son who was called Batard, and that the property has been held in that
family to this day. He also mentions the property at Butler's, as having
recently been sold.

Now, in what ship did Tristram Coffyn come to America? Of the
identity of the ship there is certainly much doubt. But it is generally
conceded that he came in the ship with Robert Clement, who settled in
Haverhill, and that Tristram first went to Salisbury. A descendant of
Robert Clement, as I am informed by letter of Robert Coffin, of Hoboken,
N. J., to William E. Coffin, of Richmond, Ind., states that the ships which
arrived in 1642, owned by Robert Clement, in which he might have come,
were the "Hector," "Griffin," "Job Clement," and "Margaret Clement."
And so, if Robert Clement arrived in one of these ships, the same must
be true of Tristram Coffyn.

It appears that he did not affect a permanent settlement at Salisbury,
but removed the same year to the new settlement of Pentucket, soon
afterward called Haverhill. This settlement was commenced in 1640,
Christopher Hussey being among the first settlers, but no deed from the
Indians was obtained until 1642, when the name of Tristram Coffyn appears as one of the witnesses thereto. It was first recorded in the county
records of Norfolk, (lib. 2, p. 209) ; and, in 1832, the original deed was
said to be in the possession of Charles White, Esq. As it is the first
appearance of the name of Tristram Coffyn upon any document in
America, I make a copy of it from the History of Haverhill by B. L.
Mirick. The marks made by the Indian sachems were representations
of the bow and arrow :

"Know all men by these presents, that wee Passaquo and Saggallew wᵗʰ
yᵉ consent of Passaconaway; have sold unto yᵉ inhabitants of Pentuckett

all ye lands wee have In Pentuckett; that is eyght myles in length from ye little Rivver in Pentuckett Westward: Six myles in length frome ye aforesaid Rivver northward: And six myles in length from ye foresaid Rivver Eastward, wth ye Ileand and ye rivver that ye ileand stand In as far in length as ye land lyes by as formerly expressed: that is, fourteene myles in length: And wee ye said Passaquo and Saggallew wth ye consent of Passaconnaway, have sold unto ye said inhabitants all ye right that wee or any of us have in ye said ground and Ileand and Rivver: And wee warrant it against all or any other Indeans whatsoever unto ye said Inhabitants of Pentuckett, and to their heires and assignes forever Dated ye fifteenth day of november Ann Dom 1642.

Witnes our hands and seales to this bargayne of sale ye day and year above written (in ye presents of us.) we ye said Passaquo & Saggallew have received In hand, for & in consideration of ye same three pounds & ten shillings:

John Ward		
	ye marke of	
Robert Clements	PASSAQUO	X [SEAL.]
Tristram Coffyn		
Hugh Sherratt		
William White		
ye signe of (l̲)	ye marke of	
Thomas Davis		
	SAGGAHEW.	X [SEAL.]

Tristram Coffyn settled in Haverhill near Robert Clement, and tradition says he was the first person who ploughed land in that town, constructing his own plough. The following year he settled at the Rocks, so called. He resided in Haverhill several years, when he removed to Newbury (1648-9), and thence to Salisbury (1654-5), where he organized the company for the purchase and settlement of Nantucket.

From the History of Newbury, by Joshua Coffin, Esq., the following extracts are made:

1644—"Tristram Coffyn is allowed to keep an ordinary, sell wine, and keep a ferry on Newbury side, and George Carr on Salisbury side of Carr's Island." (p. 43.)

"Dec. 26, 1647—Tristram Coffin (sen) is allowed to keep an ordinary and retayle wine, paying according to order, and also granted liberty to keep a ferry at Newbury side. This ferry crossed the Merrimack River at Carr's Island, George Carr keeping the Salisbury side and Tristram Coffin, sen, the Newbury side." (p. 49.)

"1653. September—Tristram Coffyn's wife, Dionis, was presented for selling beer at his ordinary, in Newbury, for three pence a quart. Having proved, upon the testimony of Samuel Mooers, that she put six bushels of malt into the hogshead she was discharged." (p. 57.)

The law which she was supposed to have violated was passed in 1645, and is as follows:

"Every person licensed to keep an ordinary, shall always be provided with good wholesome beer of four bushels of malt to the hogshead, which he shall not sell *above* two pence the ale quart, on penalty of forty shillings the first offence and for the second offence shall lose his license."

It must be remembered that this presentment was during the same period that women were presented for wearing silk hoods and scarfs and other trifling matters of dress, which were in violation of the abortive attempt to regulate the fashions of the people. Dionis doubtless intended to make a better beer than was afforded at other ordinaries; and as three pence per quart bore the same relation to six bushels of malt, as two pence per quart did to four bushels, she could see no reason why her beer should not sell for three pence per quart notwithstanding the law. Proof of this fact secured her discharge, and there can be little doubt that her beer gained a good reputation from this proceeding, and Coffyn's ordinary became distinguished as the place where the best beer was sold. It will be also noticed that Goodwife Coffyn had to bear her share of the public as well as the domestic burdens of her time.

From whatever different standpoint she was a faithful helpmeet, fitted for the necessity of an honorable race. For we cannot contemplate the dignity and moral standard maintained by every one of the children she bore, which grew to the age of maturity, nor consider the high places of distinction most of them were called to fill, nor the wreaths of honor which in their lifetimes, environed them, without becoming sensibly impressed with the truth that most great personages have rejoiced in good mothers. Although her name was not, like that of her daughter's, Mary Starbuck, associated with the public affairs of Nantucket, she was undoubtedly a woman of good judgment, and counselled with her husband in the discharge of the duties that devolved upon him in the various positions of trust which he filled. The time of her birth is not known, neither is the period of her death definitely fixed, but she survived her husband, as the probate records show.

The name Dionis is the diminutive of Dionysia, and was often written Dionys, although I cannot find that she was ever known or called in America by any other name than Dionis. It so appears in the records of Newbury and Haverhill; and in every deed of conveyance recorded in Nantucket, in which she joined her husband, it is the same. Also in the probate proceedings after the death of her husband she is there named as Dionis. It is quite remarkable that, while the name of Tristram has been perpetuated through all the generations, and in genealogical researches becomes a source of confusion it occurs so often, the name of Dionis is repeated but once in all the generations down to the present time. One grandchild only, the oldest daughter of Stephen Coffin, youngest child of Tristram and Dionis, was christened Dionis, but when she came to be married to Jacob Norton, the name appears as Dinah. It may be also stated that James Coffin had a daughter Dinah who married Nathaniel Starbuck, Jr.

So it may be said that the wife of Tristram Coffyn possessed a name that disappeared with her life, and has remained obsolete for two centuries. Yet it shall live again. In contemplating this fact I am reminded of the beautiful legend of Saint Humbert: After that good saint had been dead just a hundred years, as the story goes, his sarcophagus was opened and a sprig of laurel that had lain in burial with him during the whole century was taken from his ashes in as perfect green as if newly plucked, and fresh as if wet with the morning's dew. When the maternal progenitor of Clan Coffin was laid away to mingle with the cold clods of the valley, her laurels may have been buried with her. But as sure as eternal justice will triumph in the end—as sure as the white rose will bloom anew with every returning season, so surely will the hand of impartial history penetrate the dark portals of the tomb and lift her laurels to a glorious resurrection to bloom again green and perennial before the world, ere another century shall have been numbered with the two preceding ones of indifference and oblivion. If her name and memory be not immortalized by a figure of bronze, her life and character shall grow in the righteous estimation of her numerous descendants, till no marble or alabaster shall be found pure and white enough on which to inscribe her name.

After Tristram returned to Salisbury from Newbury he signed his name to some documents as commissioner of Salisbury. It was while a citizen of Salisbury that the plan for purchasing the island of Nantucket was conceived, and carried into practical operation.

It has been generally believed that Tristram Coffyn and his associates removed to Nantucket to escape religious persecution; and that Thomas Macy, who first removed his family hither, fled from the officers of the law, sacrificing his property and his home, rather than submit to the tyranny which punished a man for being hospitable to strangers in a rain storm, even though the strangers were Quakers. Our gifted poet Whittier has made this story almost immortal by his fine rendering of the supposed flight in a truly beautiful poem. But I must say that while his version of the affair is poetically sublime, it is historically untrue. Obed Macy's History of Nantucket indulges in this same erroneous statement, drawing conclusions therefrom, which, of course, are equally unfounded.

Thomas Mayhew was a resident of Watertown, before removing to Martha's Vineyard, and was a deputy of the General Court from that place. Thomas Macy was a deputy to the General Court from Salisbury in 1654. Mayhew's deed of the island of Nantucket from James

Fforrett, was obtained in 1641, but he did not remove to Martha's Vineyard for several years afterward. It is probable that an acquaintance was formed between Mayhew and Macy, and Tristram Coffyn (although I nowhere find that Tristram Coffyn was ever a member of the General Court from either of the towns in which he previously resided), and that Mayhew, desirous of settling the island and improving it, offered it for sale upon such terms, as will be seen by the consideration mentioned in the deed (£30 and two beaver hats), as seemed to offer opportunities for agriculture and stock raising not possible to obtain among the small settlements upon the continent, fencing being then as now a necessary expense in pursuing either occupation, and very scarce. And the very plan adopted on the island of Nantucket, of dividing and apportioning the land into commons of pasture and tillage was attempted at Newbury, in 1642, as the historian of Newbury, Joshua Coffin, states, from evidence found in Tristram Coffyn's manuscript. In his correspondence with Governor Lovelace, Thomas Macy makes allusion to Mr. Mayhew as his honored cousin.

The deed of Mayhew to the first purchasers bears date July 2, 1659, which was then the 5th month according to the old style, and the purchase was actually made as early as February of the same year, while the letter or answer of Thomas Macy to the Court respecting the offence with which he was charged of harboring Quakers, bears date 27th of 8th month, 1659, long after the purchase of the island had been consummated and the deed passed. And the said letter of Mr. Macy proves that he had never seen the men before, except one; that he did not inquire their names; and, perceiving they were Quakers, desired them to pass on, lest he might give offence by entertaining them; and assuring the Court that he had not willingly offended. Then, again, while the penalty for entertaining one of the people called Quakers, was a fine of £5 for every hour during which the Quaker was so entertained, the Court, considering the letter of Mr. Macy as a plea of guilty, imposed a nominal fine of only 30 shillings, showing that the Court did not consider the law but technically violated. It is also a matter of record that Thomas Macy went back to Salisbury and resided there in 1664, as the following extracts of a letter to a gentleman in Nantucket, written by Joshua Coffin, Esq., the historian, in 1831, will abundantly show:

" Thomas Macy was a merchant, an enlightened man, and much too wise to apprehend any danger to his person or property from any person or persons, either legally or illegally. The utmost the law could do was to fine him £4, and this sum could be mitigated according to circumstances. This was actually the case with all those who were fined for 'entertaining Quakers,' at the time Thomas Macy was fined. He stands the lowest on the list as you will find by examining the Colony records. It is there stated, Thoma Macy is fined 10s. for, &c. The idea that his property was forfeited, is no correct. It will, perhaps, be new to some people, to know that Thoma

Macy went back from Nantucket and lived in Salisbury again, and sold his land, house, &c. The record says, "Thomas Macy sold unto Anthony Colby, the house in which he, Thomas Macy, *dwelleth at the present*, together with barne and so much land as the garden conteyneth on a straight line to the eastermost corner of Roger Eastman's barne, &c.—See Registry of Deeds 1664; for in that year he lived in Salisbury. Thomas Macy never had 1000 acres of land in Salisbury. The Salisbury records state that every man worth £50 or less, shall have 4 acres of planting ground; 8 acres for £100, and so on, 4 acres for every £50. With the planting land, each settler had about double the quantity of Salt Marsh, &c. * * * * Macy was certainly a man of fortitude, courage, good sense, and education.

"James Coffin was one of the first settlers on the island in '59 or '60, but he was in Dover in 1668, and was a member of that church in 1671, and after that went back to Nantucket."

These facts are introduced for the purpose of disabusing the minds of people familiar with the general history of Nantucket and its early settlers, because it has gone into history and been generally accepted as true that the early settlers came to Nantucket because of religious persecution. And as this impression is entirely erroneous, it is important that the descendants of Tristram Coffyn, as well as the descendants of each of the other early settlers of Nantucket, should know that the first emigrations hither were purely and simply in the interest of improved homes, upon an agricultural and stock-raising basis. Neither was the island during its earliest years of white occupation that elysium which has been represented. The fathers of Nantucket did not all dwell together in unity and peace. There were local dissensions which increased with the increase of numbers, and disturbed the quietude of many homes. But, compared with the difficulties which afflicted many parts of New England, the oppressive spirit of the laws, the intolerance of religious views, the prohibitions of dress, and the Indian warfares, Nantucket was indeed blessed with "plenty's golden smile," and "a refuge of the free."

Early in 1659, according to Benjamin Franklin Folger, the most reliable genealogist of Nantucket, Tristram Coffyn proceeded upon a voyage of inquiry and observation, first to Martha's Vineyard, where he took Peter Folger, the grandfather of Dr. Benjamin Franklin, as an interpreter of the Indian language, and thence to Nantucket, his object being to ascertain the temper and disposition of the Indians, and the capabilities of the island, that he might report to the citizens of Salisbury what inducements for emigration thither were offered. I have discovered no evidence of the names of the others who accompanied him from Salisbury, but it is certain that he had others to assist in managing the boat, and very probably some of his sons, as it is a tradition, if nothing better, that James Coffin, then about 19 years old, accompanied Thomas Macy and family, Edward Starbuck, and Isaac Coleman, later in the same year, when they took up their residences upon the island.

Tristram's intercourse with the Indians was frank and [kind, and they extended to him a warm welcome. His relations with the Indians ever thereafter inspired them with confidence in his dealings as chief magistrate, and very little difficulty ever existed between the whites and the natives, a fact which was largely owing to the infusion of his liberal, high-minded and christian character into the practical concerns of life among the Indians, for it is recorded that there were some three thousand Indians upon the island when the white settlers made their abode among them, although I think that number an exaggeration.

At Martha's Vineyard he entered into preliminary negotiations with Thomas Mayhew for the purchase of the island, before visiting it, and after his visit to the island, he made additional arrangements for its purchase, and returned to Salisbury, where his report upon the condition of the island, the character of the Indians, and the advantages of a change of residence thither, was duly laid before his friends and associates. A company was organized for the immediate purchase of the whole island, allowing Thomas Mayhew to retain a one-tenth portion thereof, with some other reservations. Several meetings of the purchasers appear to have been held at Salisbury, in the summer of 1659, and general rules and regulations, for the government of the island were adopted, as the following extracts from the records made at Salisbury will show :

July 2, 1659.—These people after mentioned did buy all right and interest of the Island of Nantucket that did belong to Sr Ferdinando George and the Lord Sterling. Mr. Richard Vluet, Steward, Gentleman to Sir Ferdinando George and Mr. James Ferrett, Steward to Lord Sterling, which was by them sold unto Mr. Thomas Mayhew, of Marthers Vineyard; these after mentioned b't possess of Mr. Thomas Mayhew these Rights : namely, the patten Right belonging to the Gentleman aforesaid; and also the piece of Land which Mr. Mayhew did purchass of the Indians at the west end of the Island of Nantucket as by their grant or bill of sale, will largely appear with all the privileges and appurtenances thereof; the aforementioned Purchasers are Tristram Coffin, Senyr. Thomas Macy, Richard Swain, Thomas Barnard, Peter Coffin, Christopher Hussey, Stephen Greenleaf, John Swain, William Pile ; the said Mr. Thomas Mayhew himself also becom a Twentieth part purshaser so that they, vizt : Mr. Thomas Mayhew, Tristram Coffin, Sinr., Thomas Macy, Richard Swain, Thomas Barnard, Peter Coffin, Christopher Hussey, Stephen Greenleaf, John Swain, William Pile had the whole and Sole Interest, Disposell, power, and privilege of said Island and appurtenances thereof.

At Salysbury, February, 1659.—At a meeting of the purchasers or the major part of them appeared alowed by the rest together with some others that was owned for Ass'iates as will hereafter appear—it was agreed and Determined and approv'd as follows, vizt : that the ten owners will admitt of Ten more partners who shall have equall power and Interest with themselves, and that either of the purchasers aforementioned shall have liberty to take a partner whome he pleases not being mostly excepted against by the rest. At that meeting Robert Pike was owned partner with Christopher Hussey, Robert Barnard was owned partner with Thomas Barnard, Edwed Starbuck was oned to be Thomas Macy's partner, and Tristram Coffin, jur., partner with

Stephen Greenleaf, James Coffin partner with Peter Coffin—at the same meeting it was mutually and unanimously agreed upon, determined and concluded, that no man whatsoever shall purchase any land of any of the Indians upon the said Iland for his own private or particular use; but whatsoever purchas shall be made, shall be for the general account of the Twenty owners or purchasers and whatsoever person shall purchas any Land upon any other account, it shall be utterly void and null, except what is don by Leve from the said Owners or purchasers; at the same meeting it was ordered and Determined that there shall be ten other Inhabitants admitted into the Plantation who shall have such accomodation as the Owners or purchasers shall judge meet—as namely necessary tradesman and Seaman.

At a meeting of these owners of the Island of Nantucket at Salisbury it was Debatted, and after debatted, determed and concluded, that as there had ben a former meeting in Salisbury at the House of Benjamin Cambell, in February, 1659, in which meeting orders was made for Prohibiting of any Person from the purchasing any land from any of the Indians upon the Island of Nantucket except for the use of the Twenty owners or purchasers, the Order shall stand Inviolable unalterable as that which also as that which is likely necessary to the continuance of the well being of the place and the Conturary, that which tends to the confusion and Ruine of the whole and the Suverting of the rules and orders allready agreed upon and the deprivcing of the said owners of there Just rights and Interest. Also it was ordered at the same meeting that all the Land that is fit for areable land convenient for House lot shall be forthwith measured, that the quantity thereof may be known, which being done, shall be divided by equel proportions, that is to say Four Fifths parts to the owners or purchasers; and the other Fifth unto the Ten other Inhabitants, whereof John Bishop shall have two parts or shares, that is to say of that Fifth part belonging to the Ten Inhabitant. Also at the same meeting it was ordered that Tristram Coffin, Thomas Macy, Edward Starbuck, Thomas Barnard, Peter Folger of Mathers Vineyard, shall have power to measure and lay out said Land according to the above said awder, and whatsoever shall be done and concluded in the said Case by or any three of them, Peter Folger being one, shall be accounted Legall and valid.

May the 10th, 1661.—At a meeting at Salisbury it was ..Alered and concluded that the aforementioned parties, vizt: Tristram Coffin, seny., Thomas Macy, Edward Starbuck, Thomas Barnard, Peter Folger, shall also measure and lay out all the rest of the Land, both meadows, Woods and upland, that is convenant to be appropriated within the bounds of the first Plantation; also it is determined that the above mentioned persons, together with Mr. Mayhew, Richard Swain, John Bishop, or whatever others of the owners or purchases that are present, shall have power to Determing what land is convenient to be Improved and Laid out, and what should be common or Remain Common, and also, to Lay out the bounds of the Town and record it, provided always that the land being measured, they shall first lay out a convenant quantity of Land with suitable accomodations of all sorts which shall be Particularly reserved for the public use of the Town. Also it was ordered at the same meeting that an authentick Record shall be kept of all that is don about the proseeding and actions about the said Island, both the Island and on the main, untill further orders be taken. At the same meeting it was ordered, that for the particuler appointing which Lot every man shall have it shall be don by casting Lots excepting only those persons that have already taken there Lots, namely, Thomas Macy, Tristram Coffin, Seny., Edward Starbuck and Richard Swain.

At the same *the same* meeting Robert Pike was appointed to keep the Records concerning the Island of Nantucket at Salisbury, and Thomas Macy to keep the Records at the Island, as in the above said orders expressed at present until further orders be taken by the owners or purchasers.

Late in the season of 1659, the first of the settlers arrived, consisting of Thomas Macy and his family, Edward Starbuck, Isaac Coleman, and James Coffin. They found the natives hospitable and kind, and disposed to make them welcome. It has been often stated, and, of course, become a matter of belief, that the town was first built at Madaket, and early events are sometimes mentioned as having happened when the town was at Madaket, &c. I wish therefore to state that the town never was at Madaket, nor was there ever any considerable number of residences there. Probably there are more people living there now than at any previous time in the island's history. Macy's History of Nantucket says that Thomas Macy "chose a spot for settlement on the southeast side of Madaket harbor, where he found a rich soil and an excellent spring of water." I know not the authority for such statement, but certain it is that Tristram Coffyn first made a home near the Capaum Pond, where he resided until his death, as I shall show by quoting from the first book of records; and I also find that Thomas Macy had his house-lot laid out to the eastward of Tristram Coffyn's, near the Wanacomet Pond, in 1661. To the south and east of Capaum Pond, grew up the first village, and many of the cellar indentations where the houses stood are yet visible, as well as other evidences of human habitations.

At a meeting held at Nantucket, July 15, 1661, of the owners or purchasers residing there, it was agreed that each man have liberty to choose his house-lot within the limits not previously occupied, and that each house-lot shall contain sixty rods square to a whole share. Tristram Coffyn appears to have been allowed to make the first selection, which is recorded as follows, together with the other lots:

[FROM FIRST BOOK OF NANTUCKET RECORDS.]

Tristram Coffin, Sen., had his house lot layed out at Cappammet, by the aforesaid Lot layers, at Cappammet Harbour head, sixty rods squar, or thereabouts, the east side line part of it bounded by the highway; the south side bounded by a rock southward of the pond; the north by the harbour head; the west side bounded by the lot of Tristram Coffin, Jr., more or less, as it is layd out.

Peter Coffin had his house lot layd out by the aforesaid lot layers on the East side of Cappammet harbour, the *Nake* [neck] of Land lying between the said harbour and the pond commonly called the whale pond, bounded by a rock at the southwest corner; and from thence on a straight line to the east side of the aforesaid pond; the bound is the end of the neck so far as the upland goes, more or less.

Tristram Coffin, Junior, had his house lot layd out by the aforesaid Lot layers at Coppammet, sixty rods squar, or thereabouts, on the east side by the lot of his father, Tristram Coffin; on the south side by the common; on the west by the lot of William Pile, more or less, as it is layed out.

James Coffin had his house lot layed out by the aforesaid lot layers, sixty rods squar, or thereabouts, bounded on the south by the lot of Nathaniel Starbuck; the West side bounded by the common; on the East by the land of Stephen Greenleaf, more or less.

The one half of the accomodation to Tristram Coffin, sen., being assigned to Mary Starbuck and Nathaniel Starbuck, Tristram also being present at the place commonly called the Parliament House, Sixty rod square, bounded with the land of Thos. Mayhew on the south; and with the land of James Coffin on the north; and on the east with the land of Stephen Greenleaf; on the west by the common—Same land allowed at the east end with reference to rubbage land, more or less.

Tristram Coffin, sen., had an acre of meadow lay out by Edw'd Starbuck, Thos. Macy, himself being present, and Peter Folger agreeing thereto, on the nack commonly called Nanna hamak Neck, at the south end of the wood-layd. At the same time Tristram Coffin, junior, had an acre lot laid out at the same place. At the same time Peter Coffin had a lot layed out, one acre, bounded with the lot of Tristram Coffin, Jr., on the southwest, and with the lot of Tristram Coffin on the northwest.

Tristram Coffin, Sen., had a twenty acre lot; being a Second Division answerable to the lot laid out in the five pound purchases, thirty rod in breadth, lying a Long from the north side of the house lot of the said Tristram Coffin lot, by Cuppammet head to the sea, more or less.

Tristram Coffin, Jr., had twenty acre lot layed out by Tristram Coffin, Edward Starbuck & Peter Folger, answerable to the twenty acres on the five pound purches.

Tristram Coffyn was thirty-seven years of age upon his removal to America, and fifty-five years of age at the time of his removal to Nantucket, having spent eighteen years in America previous to his coming to the island to reside. It does not appear that his mother, Joan Coffyn, ever resided in Nantucket; and it does appear that she died in Boston, in May, 1661, at the age of 77 years; the Rev. Mr. Wilson, who preached the funeral sermon, spoke of her as a woman of extraordinary character. Mirick's History of Haverhill, quoting from Sewall's Diary, which recorded the fact of Joan Coffyn's death, says he "embalmed her memory." Of his two sisters who came with him to America, Eunice married William Butler, and Mary married Alexander Adams, whose history cannot here be further followed up. And of his two sisters, Joan and Deborah, who were married in England before his departure for America, nothing has ever been definitely ascertained.

Three of his children, viz., Peter, Tristram, Jr., and Elizabeth, were married at the time of his removal to Nantucket. Elizabeth married Stephen Greenleaf, November 13, 1651, while they were living at New-bury, the first grandchild being Stephen Greenleaf, Jr., born August 15, 1652. This grandchild well remembered his great-grandmother, Joan Coffyn, and lived to see his own great-grandchildren. I do not find that Stephen Greenleaf or Tristram Coffin, Jr., ever removed their families to or became residents of Nantucket, although they were of the original purchasers. Peter Coffin, however, became a resident of the island. Tristram, senior, did not remove his entire family until 1662.

From the early historical and traditional accounts Tristram Coffyn was the leading spirit among the islanders at the commencement of the settlement, and the interests which he and his sons and sons-in-law represented (for he frequently signed his name in matters of proprietorship for himself and five others), gave him power to control in a great degree the enterprises of the island. During the first years of his residence upon the island he was the richest proprietor, except his son, Peter, who was reputed to be possessed of great estate. It is not to be found, however, that he ever exercised his power unduly for his own advantage. He sought to have his associates purchase jointly with him the island of Tuckernuck. Failing to enlist them in his further enterprise, he, with his three eldest sons, made a purchase of it in their own right. When the man to whom certain rights had been granted upon condition that he maintain a mill for grinding the grain produced by the islanders failed to construct the same, it was Tristram Coffyn that assumed the contract and built and maintained the mill. In all the Indian troubles (for the aborigines were simply North American Indians), our common ancestor held them in subjection in such manner as commanded their respect. He employed large numbers of them in his farming operations, and built them improved wigwams upon his land. Our late most valued historian, Benjamin Franklin Folger, speaking of his relation to the Indians says: "The christian character which he exhibited and which he practically illustrated in all the varied circumstances and conditions of that infant colony, is analogous to that which subsequently distinguished the founder of Pennsylvania, so that the spirit of the one seemed to be but the counterpart of the other."

The Indians were divided into bands and sometimes had quarrels among themselves and sometimes were at variance with the whites. Whether the white man was always the aggressor, as has been asserted quite confidently by the philanthropic friends of the Indian in later times, cannot be decided; but one thing may be stated without fear of contradiction, that the Indians became troublesome only after they had learned to drink rum, and rum was introduced among them by the whites. The early court records are mainly devoted to trials, convictions, and sentences of Indians to be whipped for getting drunk and for petty larcenies; and of fines imposed upon white men and women for selling rum to Indians. Strong drink was the bane of the Nantucket Indians, and, so marked were its demoralizing influences, that the first General Court for Nantucket and Martha's Vineyard, composed of Tristram Coffyn, first chief magistrate of Nantucket, and Thomas Mayhew, first chief magistrate of Martha's Vineyard, and two associates from

each island, enacted a law prohibiting the sale of intoxicating drinks to
Indians. It is probably the first prohibitory liquor law on record. The
evil of rum drinking among the Indians became a serious matter, and
the prohibitory measures had a restraining influence; yet for the love of
gain, white men then, as now, violated the law and sold rum to the Indians. The law was occasionally enforced, however, and John Gardner,
whose gravestone alone marks the spot where our ancestors were first
interred, complained to Governor Lovelace, at New York, under date of
March 15, 1676, that a half barrel of rum had been taken from him by
Thomas Macy, then chief magistrate. Mr. Gardner also represented
that the Indian Sachems said they would fight if the laws against them
were enforced.

Without entering into the consideration of all the causes which led to
the personal and partisan difficulties between the white settlers at this
time, it is clear that rum-drinking among the Indians was one great
cause; and the letter of Thomas Macy to Governor Lovelace, bearing
date of May 9, 1676, amply shows the fear he entertained of the Indians
if strong drink was allowed to be sold them. And he asks the Governor
to make an order prohibiting any vessel that shall come into the harbor
from selling strong drink to Indians, believing that an order from the
Governor at New York would have more force than laws enacted by the
magistrates. He uses this strong language: "Sir, concerning the Peace
we hitherto enjoy, I cannot imagine it could have bin if strong Liquor
had bin among the Indians, as formerly; for my owne yt I have been to
ye utmost an opposed of the Trade these 38 yeares, and I verily be-
lieve (respecting the Indians) tis the only Ground of the miserable
p'sent Ruine to both Nations; for tis that hath kept them from Civility,
they have been the drunken Trade kept all the while like wild Beares
and Wolves in the Wildernesse."

It also appears that the Court on one occasion took possession of all
the liquor upon the island and disposed of it in small quantities as the
owners and English neighbors had need of.

The appointment of Tristram Coffyn as the first chief magistrate of
Nantucket, was about the same time that Thomas Mayhew was appointed
the first chief magistrate of Martha's Vineyard. The commission bears
date 29th of June, 1671. The two chiefs, together with two assistants
from each island, were to constitute a General Court with appellate jurisdiction over both islands. It appears that Governor Lovelace desired
the inhabitants to recommend two suitable persons for chief magistrate,
for him to make a selection from. They named Tristram Coffyn and
Thomas Macy, and he made choice of the former.

The town voted to have a harrow for the use of the inhabitants; and
they further voted that Mr. Tristram Coffyn provide the harrow, and that

A2

he and Mr. Thomas Macy be empowered to see that every man sowed seed " according to order."

The first commission of Mr. Tristram Coffyn to be chief magistrate, is copied *verbatim* from the third book of Deeds, page 62, in the Secretary's Office at Albany, by Mr. F. B. Hough, and is as follows:

Commission granted to Mr. Tristram Coffin, Senr., to be Chief Magistrate in and over the Islands of Nantuckett and Tuckanuckett.

[Deeds lii, 62, Secretary's Office.]

Francis Lovelace, Esq., &c.: Whereas upon address made unto mee by Mr. Tristram Coffin and Mr. Thomas Macy on ye behalfe of themselves and ye rest of ye Inhabitants of Nantuckett Island concerning ye Mannor and Method of Government to be used amongst themselves, and having by ye advice of my councell pitcht upon a way for them; That is to say, That they be governed by a person as Chiefe Magistrate, and two Assistants, ye former to be nominated by myselfe, ye other to be chosen and confirmed by ye Inhabitants as in ye Instructions sent unto them is more particularly sett forth. And having conceived a good opinion of ye fitness and capacity of Mr. Tristram Coffin to be ye present Chiefe Magistrate to manage affayres with ye Ayd and good advice of ye Assistants in ye Islands of Nantuckett and Tuckanuckett, I have thought fit to nominate, constitute, and appoint, and by these presents doe hereby nominate, constitute and appoint Mr. Tristram Coffin to be Chief Magistrate of ye said Islands of Nantuckett and Tuckanuckett. In ye management of which said employment hee is to use his best skill and endeavour to preserve his Maties Peace and to keep ye Inhabitants in good Order. And all Persons are hereby required to give ye said Mr. Tristram Coffin such respect and obedience as belongs to a Person invested by commission from authority of his Royall Highness in ye place and employment of a Chiefe Magistrate in ye Islands aforesaid. And hee is duly to observe the Orders and Instructions which are already given forth for ye well governing of ye Place; or such others as from time to time shall hereafter bee given by mee : And for whatsoever ye said Mr. Tristram Coffin shall lawfully Act or Doe in Prosecution of ye Premises, This my Commission which is to bee of fforce until ye 13th day of October, which shall bee in ye yeare of our Lord, 1672, when a new Magistrate is to enter into the employment shall be his sufficient Warrant and Discharge.

Given under my Hand and Seale at fforte James, in New Yorke, this 29th day of June, in ye 22d yeare of his Maties Reigne, Annoq Dni. 1671.

FRAN. LOVELACE.

There existed a feud in 1675–6, between Thomas Macy, chief magistrate, and William Worth, his son-in-law, of one party, and John Gardner and Peter Folger and others, of the other party. The commission of Mr. Macy had run out, and, no successor being appointed, Mr. Macy continued to act. Peter Coffin had returned to the island from Boston, and was chosen an associate magistrate. The method of choosing was by ballot of corn and beans. All in favor of electing Peter Coffin were to vote corn, and those opposed were to vote beans. There must have been considerable electioneering in those days about the Old Parliament House, for one enthusiastic advocate of Peter Coffin's election exclaimed "Corn Peter Coffin! If he don't serve we will get his fine." It was objected that Peter Coffin already held a commission in Boston and was Deputy of the General Court of Massachusetts and could not legally serve; but, notwithstanding all objections, he was chosen. His election seemed to have been a triumph of the young men over the older ones. For Peter Folger, in his letter of complaint to Governor Andross, at New York, speaks rather contemptuously of "our new young magistrates." Peter Folger was the clerk of the Court, and refused to perform the functions required of him by the chief magistrate. Whereupon he was put under arrest. Thomas Macy issued the following summons, signing it himself:

"'Tis the order of the Court that the Constable be sent to Peter Ffoulger for the Court Booke, and all the Records of that Nature, and this is to impower the Constable herein to bring them to ye Court forthwith, and Peter Ffoulger is hereby required to deliver them.
Pr me,   Tho: Macy, Mag."

Mr. Folger came to the Court, but he answered not. William Worth was chosen clerk of the Court, and the following indictment was found against Peter Folger for contempt:

At a Court of Ajurment held in the Towne of Sherburne, 14th Febulary, 1676 Petter Foulger, Inditted for Contempt of his Magis Athority, in not appearing before the Court according to sumons serued on him and being Aprehended by Specall Warrant being braoft to the Court to Aufwer for his Contentious Carage, And being demanded why he did fo act gaue no Anfwer: Th'o the Court waited on hem a While and vrged him to fpeak, The Sentence of the Court is to Remite the Caufe to the Court of Afize at New York as the law derects and to giue twenty Pound Bond for his appearance, and to abide the Order of the Court and to ftand comitted ti'l Bond be given.
A true Copy By the Court
William Worth, Cl.

Mr. Folger not finding bondsmen was placed in prison. He describes it as "A place where never any Englishman was put, and where the Neighbors Hoge had layd but the Night before, and in a bitter cold Frost and deep Snow. They had only thrown out most of the Durt, Hoge Dung and Snow. The Rest the Constable told me I might ly upon if I would, that is upon the Boards in that Case, and without Victuals or Fire. Indeed I perswaded him to fetch a little Hay, and he did so, and some Friend did presently bring in some Beding and Victuals."

· The people generally took sides upon the matters in controversy, and a bitter feeling was engendered. The admission of new partners into the arrangements for settling and utilizing the island introduced an element of discord; and, the Province of New York claiming and holding jurisdiction of the island, there grew up a feeling in favor of accepting the jurisdiction of the Massachusetts Province. Under this high state of feeling, upon a representation of the affairs at New York, Governor Andross, who had succeeded Governor Lovelace, called Tristram

Coffyn again to the chief magistracy. While Tristram was the senior of Thomas Macy by only three years, yet, by virtue of his numerous family, he appears to have been regarded as the patriarch of the island; and when this great dissention among the settlers had assumed proportions alarming to the better angels of their nature, they instinctively turned to Tristram Coffyn as the one man who could administer justice to the islanders with impartiality. Yet he did not altogether succeed, as we shall subsequently see. The second commission as chief magistrate is copied from the Nantucket Records, and is as follows:

Second Commission of Tristram Coffin to be Chief Magistrate.

[1st book Nantucket Records, page 101.]

Edmund Andros, Esqr., seigneur of Sausmarez, Lieut. & Governour General under his Royall Highnesse James, Duke of Yorke and Albany, &c., of all his Territories in America:

Whereas an undue or illegall returne of the Chief Magistrate of Nantuckett hath been made two yeares successively from thence, the one being by law wholly incapable thereof: Therefore by advice of my Counsell, by vertue of his Majesties Letters Pattents, & authority from his Royall Highnesse, I doe hereby in his Majesty's name, nominate, constitute, and authorize Mr. Tristram Coffin, senr., to be Chiefe Magistrate of the said Island of Nantucket and dependencyes for the ensuing yeare, or further order, in the place and stead of Mr. Thomas Macy, late Chiefe Magistrate, and being thereunto sworn by him, or next in place, to act as Chiefe Magistrate according to Law and lawfull custome and practice, requiring all persons whom it may concern, to conform themselves thereunto accordingly.

Given under my hand and seale of the Province in New Yorke, this sixteenth day of September 1677.

E. ANDROSS.

In another book, the text evidently written by Peter Coffin, before whom it was acknowledged, is the following oath of office taken by Tristram Coffyn, to which his autograph is annexed. It is the only trace of his own hand found upon any of the records:

[Book 2—in Register of Deeds Office, Nantucket.]

Whereas I, Tristram Coffin, senior, have Received a Com'n baring date the 16 of September, 1677, Investinge me with power to be chefe magistrate one the ITd of Nantucket and dependances, for this ye one yeare ensuinge, or til further order, I, Tristram Coffin, above said, doe engage my selfe, under the penalty of perjury, to doe Justise in all causes that come before me, according to law and endeavor to my best understanding and heareunto I have subscribed

TRISTRAM COFFYN, chefe magstrat.

Mr. Tristram Coffin, senior, acknowledged this above subscription to be his Act and deed Before me

PETER COFFIN, Assistant.

Soon after the marriage of Mary Coffin, the youngest daughter of Tristram, with Nathaniel Starbuck, the old gentleman concluded to make his son-in-law a landed proprietor; and, with as much care for the contingencies of the future as kind parents exercise in the present age, and with equal nicety in the choice of language as may be found in modern conveyances, executed the following deed to his daughter and her husband. It will be seen that it was made some years before it was acknowledged, and acknowledged some years before it was recorded:

Tristram conveys to daughter Mary Starbuck and her husband Nathaniel 1-2 of all estates.

[Nantucket Records, 1st Book, Page 97.]

Know all Men by these Presents, that I, Tristram Coffin, of Nantucket, do for divers good considerations, as Also in regard of my Fatherly affections, do give unto my daughter, Mary Starbuck, the one half of my accomodation of my purchase, on Nantucket Island, namely, the half of my tenth part which I bought with the other nine first purchasers of Mr. Thomas Mayhew, in Patten right, and of the Shachems Indians right, as by there grant in the Deed will at large appeare: I do as aforesaid give and grant unto my daughter, Mary Starbuck, all the one he'? of my accomodation of Patten Right, and all my Right of the half of all lands, Meadows, marshes, commons, Timber, wood, and all appurtenances Thereunto belonging, as fully as myself or any of the other Twenty part shares have or ought to have, in manner and form following: the one half to her own and her Husband's Disposal, namely, her Husband, Nathaniel Starbuck, to them and their heirs and assigns, forever, the other half to my aforesaid Daughter, Mary Starbuck, and Nathaniel Starbuck, her Husband, during their Lives, and when they Dy, then it shall be for the use of my Daughter, Mary Starbuck's child, or children, to him, her, or them, and their heirs, forever; but, if my Daughter, Mary Starbuck, have no child or children Living when she Dyeth, Then it shall be in the power of her Husband, Nathaniel Starbuck, to Dispose of all the aforesaid Lands and Accomodations, with all appurtenances, as he shall Judge most meet. in witness whereof, I, the said Tristram Coffin, have hereunto set my hand and seal, this 14th 4th mo, 1664.

TRISTRAM COFFYN.

[Signed sealed and delivered in the presence of—
THOMAS MACY,
MARY SWAIN,
SARAH MACY.

This deed was acknowledged before me, Thomas Mayhew, upon the Island of Nantucket, this 15th day of January, 1677, I say before me

THOMAS MAYHEW, Mag.

July 26, 1736.—Then Receiv'd the original of this above written Deed, and by the Desire of same conserned, perfected the Record above by making the sign of the seal. Attest: ELEZER FOLGER, Regr.

While Tristram was generally reputed to be quite wealthy in goods and lands, owning, together with his sons, at one time about a one-fourth part of the island of Nantucket, and the whole of Tuckernuck, he did not die rich. He fully realized that he could not take his riches with him to another world, and that the amount of land he would require at his death would be very small. He made no will, but disposed of much of his land while he lived, by deeds, the consideration always being his "regard and natural affection." Most of the remainder of his estate he deeded to his two youngest sons, John and Stephen, and they were to take after the decease of both himself and his wife. To each of his grandchildren he gave ten acres of land upon the island of Tuckernuck, or to such of them as would plant it.

Tristram to Stephen, his youngest son, conveying half his accommodations, excepting his new house on the hill.

[Nantucket Records, Old Book, Page 63.]

Know all Men by these presents, that I, Tristram Coffin, of Nantucket, Senore, do give, grant, bargain and sell unto my son, Stephen Coffin, the one-half of my land at Cappam, Alies Northam, within the township of Sherborn, situated upon Nantucket Island, that is to say, the one half of my house lot with half my accomodations and privileges and appurtenances whatsoever thereunto belonging, all building except, that is to say, my new dwelling house upon the hill, and my old dwelling house under the hill, by the Erbe garden; now, for and in consideration of the aforesaid premisses, my son, Stephen Coffin, shall always from time to time do the best he can in managing of my other half of my lands and accomodation, during mine and my wife's life, and that he be helpfull to me and his mother in our old age and sickness, what he can : now I, Tristram Coffin, above said, do for this and for divers other considerations me moving thereunto, do as above said, give, grant, bargain, and sell unto my son, Stephen Coffin, his heirs and assigns, all my one half of my house lot with all appurtenances thereunto belonging : To have and to hold forever, to him, the said Stephen Coffin, his heirs and assigns, executors and administrators, upon the conditions aforesaid ; and my son, Stephen Coffin, shall allways from time to time, have free liberty to go to and froe to the new barne that he hath lately built with horse, foot, and cart, as he hath occasion, and to have the free use of half an acre of land adjoining the said Barn on the East side, and South and North side. in witness whereof, I have set my hand and seal, the fifteenth of the eleventh mone, one thousand six hundred and seventy-six.   TRISTRAM COFFYN.

Acknowledged before me the deed within written this 15th day of June, 1677.   THOMAS MAYHEW, Magistrate.

Agreement between Stephen Coffin and his father, as to rights in barn to Tristram and his wife Dionis.

[Nantucket Records, 2d Book, Page 12.]

Artickels of agreement between Tristram Coffin, Senior, and Stephen Coffin, Son of the aforesaid Tristram Coffin, both of the Town of Sherborn, on the Island of Nantucket, as followeth : imprimis, we do Jointly and severally agree that whereas there is a Barn built at Coppamet by us, this present year, one Thousand Six hundred seventy seven, that the aforesaid Stephen Coffin hath bin at the most part of the charge, therefore I, Tristram Coffin, do covenant and agree with my son, Stephen

Coffin, that he shall have the aforesaid barn and Lentors for himself, and his heirs and assigns, forever: To have and to hold and Quietly to Injoy, in Consideration whereof, as also in Consideration of the Receiving of Two Thousand foot of boards, and some Timber, and some Labour of severall persons in framing the works, I, Stephen Coffin, do Consent and agree that my Father, Tristram Coffin, and my mother, Dionis Coffin, shall have the use of the one half of the aforesaid barn, Coming in and going to the barn and Lentors without any kind of hindrance, Let, or molestation, by, from, or under me, Stephen Coffin, my heirs, executors, Administrators, or Assigns; and if my Father and Mother aforesaid do happen to Dye in some short time, as namely, within seven years after the Date hereof, then I, Stephen Coffin, do engage to pay the some of Ten Pounds to my Father or Mother's order, within one year after their Decease, if they or either of them order me so to do. Witness our hands and seals to this agreement, the 18th of July, 1677.

Signed, sealed, and delivered in presence of us,
  who are witness to these present within
  written artickles of agreement:
  MARTHA HUSSEY,   THOMAS MACY,
  NATHANIEL BARNARD.

TRISTRAM COFFYN,
STEPHEN COFFIN.

this Deed was Acknowledged this 24th Day of July before me
                      THOS. MACY, Mag.

Tristram grants his new dwelling house to his son John.
[Nantucket Records, 2d Book, Page 19.]

To all christian people To whome these presents shall come, Tristram Coffin, Senior, in the Town of Sherborn, on the Island of Nantucket, sendeth greeting, and Declareth that, in regard to my naturall afections unto my son, John Coffin, now of Sharbon, as also for divers other good and Lawful consideration, I, the above said Tristram Coffin, do freely give unto my son, John Coffin, and to his heirs, forever, my new Dwelling house, with all other houses Adjoining unto it, and also the whole half share of land and accomodation and appurtenances thereunto Belonging, Namly, my part of the House lot and all commonage of Timber, wood, pasturages, and all mendows, marshes, and creek grass thereunto belonging, the aforesaid Tristram Coffin, do freely and firmly by these, give, grant, and confirm the above said Dwelling House, with all privileges and appurtenances as afore named, unto my son, John Coffin, and to his heirs: to have and to hold forever, imediatly after the Decease of me, the aforesaid Tristram Coffin, Senior, and my now wife, Dionis Coff'n, free and discharged against all persons or person laying any claim unto the above said House or any appurtenances thereunto belonging, in, by, or under me; and in witness hereof, I, Tristram Coffin, Senior, have set my hand and seal, the third Day of December, one Thousand Six hundred Seventy Eight.

                    TRISTRAM COFFYN, Senior.

Witness hereunto:
  JAMES COFFIN,
  STEPHEN COFFIN.

This was acknowledged by Mr. Tristram Coffin to be his act and Deed the 3d 10 m, 1678.

                WILLIAM WORTH, Assistant.
A true copy: WILLIAM WORTH, Recorder.

Tristram grants ten acres of land to each of his grandchildren to plant.

[Nantucket Records, 2d Book, Page 17.]

All Men shall know by these presents, that I, Tristram Coffin, of Sherborn, on the Island of Nantucket, with or in Regard of my Natural afection unto my Grand Children, I do freely give unto every one of them Ten Acres of land to plant or sow English grain on, or any other Improvement for oats or what is fit for food for men. I say I, the above said Tristram Coffin, senior, do freely and fermly give unto all and every one of my grand children that are now living, or that shall be born hereafter, each of them ten acres of Land upon the Island of Tuckernuck: To have and to hold to plant Indian Corn or to sow or plant any other grain on, and if they or any of them shall sow their land with english hay seed they shall have liberty to keep four shep upon every acre during *dureing* their Life time, of any one that shall so improve the above named Land, or any part of it. in Witness hereof, I, Tristram Coffin, have set my hand and seal 3d 10th 1678.

Signed, sealed and delivered in presence of us
the within written Deed.   } TRISTRAM COFFYN.
    JAMES COFFIN,   JOHN COFFIN,
      STEPHEN COFFIN.

This Deed was acknowledged by Mr. Tristram Coffin to be his act and Deed before me WILLIAM WORTH, assestant 3 m 10th 1678.

this is a true copy of the origenall by me—WILLIAM WORTH, Regr.,

By these deeds above quoted we shall learn that Tristram Coffyn had a new dwelling house, which stood on a hill, and another dwelling house which stood under the hill. Also, that he last lived in his new house on the hill. With this information, and by tracing the title of the new house on the hill, which was conveyed to John Coffin, and from John to his son Peter, and from Peter to his son Robert, the said Robert's estate being defined within the recollection of the present generation, I think we can know the exact spot where Tristram Coffyn last resided, and from which place his mortal put on immortality. His wife, who survived him, doubtless breathed her last in the same mansion, as she was to have a life right carved out of the estate which subsequently became vested in John and Stephen Coffin. The Court of Sessions, at that time exercising probate jurisdiction, allowed to Mrs. Dionis Coffyn the use of the entire estate of her husband during her life, the three sons, James, John, and Stephen, as administrators, so recommending.

The date of Tristram's death has been fixed by some writers as having occurred on the 2d day of October, 1681, and I have given it as such in the opening paragraph of this book. It is so recorded in the record of deaths in the Town Clerk's office. But in the Records of the Court held the month following his death, where his three sons, then residing upon the island, appeared and were granted letters of administration, it is plainly written 3d. And on the 8th day of the following August, when an inventory of the estate was presented, the date of his death is again stated as occurring on the *third* day of October, and this time it is spelled out. So that the preponderance of record evidence is in favor of the 3d of October, 1681. It is possible that the death occurred at midnight, about the close of the 2d and commencement of the 3d, and the time differently estimated by different persons. The night of the 2d would be continuous with many at that time, until the daylight of the 3d, and timepieces were not as numerous as now, the hour-glass serving principally as a recorder of time.

The following copies from the Court records will reveal the condition of his estate at the time of his decease, and the proceedings had thereon. It was the last service performed for him by his children, and was done decently and in order:

Mr. James Coffin, John Coffin, Steven Coffin doe bind ourselves, Joyntly and severally, in the some of an hundred pounds starlinge, to perform the trust in administering on our father's estate, and to baer the Court harmless according to law.

JAMES COFFIN,
JOHN COFFIN,
STEPHEN COFFIN.

At a Court of Sessions held the 29th of November, 1681, I have granted administration unto Mr. James Coffin, John Coffin and Steven Coffin, on the estate of Mr. Tristram Coffin, deceased the 3d day of October, 1681, tne having given security according to law.

The 8th day of August, 1682, an inventory being presented to the Court of the estate of Mr. Tristram Coffin, senior, who departed this life the third day of October, on thousand six hundred eighty one, the Court taking into consideration the present state of the estate, together with the best information of his mind before his decease; doe order the use of the estate for Mrs Dionis Coffin, his widdow, during her life, after al just debts are paid.

At a Court this 9th February, 1682.

Mr. James Coffin and Steven Coffin appeared at this Court desiring discharg of further standing administrator to the estate of Tristram Coffin, deceased. It appeared to the Court they having made payment of all the estate.

As previously indicated, Tristram assumed the duties of Chief Magistrate the last time under peculiar circumstances. He succeeded his long time friend and associate Thomas Macy, against whom there had been bitter animosities engendered. The difficulties which perplexed Mr. Macy, also annoyed Tristram. And while it does not appear that he was interested in the contentions to the extent that Mr. Macy was, yet as his interests were the same, it is nowise probable that his opinions were withheld. He adhered to the policy maintained by the twenty original purchasers, as opposed to the claims of the subsequent settlers who were admitted to certain privileges and accorded certain rights specifically mentioned, but not upon terms of equality. The new settlers were allowed half shares upon certain conditions; but they multiplied and soon outnumbered the original band, and partisan feelings were fostered, and jealousies appealed to in such manner, that the era of good feeling was passed never more to be recalled in his day, if ever after enjoyed. His last administration, as will be discovered by the official documents presented, was not without its alloy of unhappiness, and left him a legacy of sorrow, which his sons, with filial regard, hastened to relieve him of. In his humble petition for relief, he touchingly refers to the act of his son having saved him from languishing in a prison; and to John Gardner, his successor as chief magistrat, who presented his petition, as his loving neighbor.   •

The official act which caused him to sacrifice his property to repair, was one of omission rather than commission. A ship was wrecked on Nantucket shoals, in September, 1678, loaded with hides, and the chief magistrate allowed her to be wrecked by parties. Portions of the cargo and rigging were embezzled. A Court of Admiralty held the chief magistrate responsible, and the parties who had derived the benefit of wrecking the vessel refused to bear any share of the fine, and the burden fell upon Tristram Coffyn alone. His own testimony in the case seems to have been all the evidence against him upon which the decision was made up. No one of his descendants will read the story as officially recorded, without a feeling of pride that their great ancestor, under a most distressing ordeal, in which both his fortune and his honor were at stake, saved his honor. And the Governor at New York discharged him from the award of the Admiralty upon his representation.

Through these documents, preserved for more than two centuries, we get a glimpse of the spirit of the times which our Nantucket ancestors impressed with their own personality. And, while the first settlers were not all agreed upon the subjects of public policy which subsequently entered into the political concerns of the island, and while their dissentions oftentimes assumed a degree of acrimony and vindictiveness painful to reflect upon, they were very generally men of sturdy character and heroic lives. Looking back through the dim vista of two hundred years we shall behold a galaxy of names illumined by high resolves—names that have not tarnished with time nor faded from the world with the friction of the centuries—names that were not born to die. We shall see engraven high up on the world's escutcheon the names. of Macy, Starbuck, Folger, Gardner, Swain, Hussey, Coleman, Barnard—and then, still higher up, resplendent with innumerable descending rays.

of light and love and christian sympathy, extending throughout the broad universe, we shall see the name of Tristram Coffyn.

At the age of 76 he passed from the scenes of earth, honored and respected by a large race of descendants, and numerous friends and neighbors. At his death he left a posterity of 7 children, 60 grandchildren, and a number of great-grandchildren. His posterity is more numerous now. In 1722 there had been born 1138 descendants, of whom 871 were then living. In 1728, six years later, there had been added to the number born 444, making the total number born 1582; and of that number 1128 still survived. This computation, by Stephen Greenleaf, the first grandchild, was made more than one hundred and fifty years ago. What the number now is will never be definitely ascertained. Their name is legion.

The ancestor Tristram found a sepulchre upon the island of Nantucket where he died, but none of his numerous descendants can point out the place. If the old cemetery east of the Maxey's pond was used for burial as early as 1681, he was doubtless interred therein. If not, then most likely upon his own estate.

Nantucket being a dependency of the Province of New York, the earliest records concerning the island are found among the archives of that State, at Albany. From these official records Mr. Franklin B. Hough, in 1856, made a compilation of very many valuable and exceedingly interesting documents relating to Nantucket, which would probably never have seen the light but for his labors. They are printed in a small book, and though the number of copies printed was limited to one hundred and fifty, I have been enabled to possess myself of one long enough to make the following extracts therefrom:

Deeds from James Fforrett to Thomas Mayhew and Son.
[Deeds, 1, 71; III, 64, and III, 76, Secretary's Office, Albany.]

Thefe Prefents doe witneffe, That I, James Fforrett, Gent., who was fent over into thefe parts of America, by the Honble Lord Sterling with a Commiffion for the ordering and difpofing of all the Iflands that lyeth between Cape Codd and Hudfons River, and have hitherto continued his Agent without any Contradiction, doe hereby graunt unto Thomas Mayhew at Watertowne, Merchant, and to Thomas Mayhew his Soune, free Liberty and full Power to them, their Heyres and Affignes, to Plant and Inhabitt upon Nantuckett and two finall Iflands adjacent, and to enjoy the faid Iflands to them, their Heyres, and Affignes forever. Provided, That Thomas Mayhew and Thomas Mayhew his Soune or either of them or their Affignus doe render and pay yearly unto the Honble the Lord Sterling, his Heyres and Affignes, fuch an Acknowledgement as fhall bee thought fitt by John Winthrop Efqr the Elder, or any two Magiftrates in the Maffachufetts Bay, being chofen for that End and Purpofe by the Hon. the Lord Sterling or his Deputy; and by the faid Thomas Mayhew and Thomas Mayhew his Soune, or their Affignes.

Its agreed, That the Governmt that the faid Thomas Mayhew and Thomas Mayhew his Soune and their Affinees fhall fett up, fhall bee fuch as is now eftablifhed in the Maffachufetts aforefaid, and that the faid Thomas Mayhew and Thomas Mayhew his Soune and their Affigues fhall have as much Priviledge touching their Planting, Inhabitting, and Enjoying, of all and every Part of the Premifes as by the Patent to the Patentees of the Maffachufetts aforefaid, and their Affociates. In Witneffe hereof I the faid James Fforrett have hereunto fett my Hand and Seale this 13th Day of October, 1641.

JAMES FFORRETT (Seale)

Witneffes :
ROBERT CORANE.
NICHOLAS DAVISON,
Richd STILLMAN.

PHILIP WATSON, Clerke.

A Deed Made to Mr. Mayhew by Richard Vines.

[Deeds, iii, 66, Secretary's Office.]

I, Richard Vines, of Saco. Gent., Steward Gen^{rll} for Sir Fferdinand Gorges, K^{nt}, Lord Proprietor of ye Province of Mayne Land and ye Iflands of Caparrock and Nantican, doe by thefe Prefents give full Power and Authority unto Thomas Mayhew, Gent: his Heyres and Affociates, to plant and Inhabitt upon ye Iflands of Caparrock als Martha's Vineyard, wth all Rights and Priveledges thereunto belonging, to enjoy the Premifes unto himfelfe his Heyres and Affociates forever, yielding and paying unto ye faid Sr Ferdinand Gorges, his Heyres and Alllgnes forever annually, as two Gent. Indifferently by each of them chofen, fhall judge to be meet by way of acknowledgment.

Given under my Hand this 25th day of October, 1641.

RICH^d VINES.

Witnefs :
THOMAS PAGE,
ROBERT LONG.

Deed of Nantucket to Ten Purchafers.

[Deeds iii, 56, Secretary's Office.]

Recorded for Mr. Coffin and Mr. Macy aforefd ye Day and Yeareaforefd .

Bee it known unto all Men by thefe Prefents, that I, Thomas Mayhew, of Martha's Vineyard, Merchant, doe hereby acknowledge, that I have sould unto Triftram Coffin, Thomas Macy, Chriftopher Huffey, Richard Swayne, Thomas Bernard, Peter Coffin, Stephen Greenleafe, John Swagne, and William Pike, that Right and Intereft I have in ye Land of Nantuckett, by Patent; ye wch Right I bought of James Fforrett, Gent. and Steward to ye Lord Sterling, and of Richard Vines fometimes of Sacho, Gent.. Steward-Gen^{rll} unto Sir Georges, Knight, as by Conveyances under their Hands and Seales doe appeare, ffor them ye aforefaid to Injoy, and their Heyres and Alllgnes forever, wth all the Priviledges thereunto belonging, for in confideration of ye Sume of Thirty Pounds of Current Pay, unto whomfoever I ye faid Thomas Mayhew, mine Heyres or Alllgnes, fhall appoint. And alfo two Beaver Hatts, one for myfelfe, and one for my wife. And further, this is to declare that I the faid Thomas Mayhew have received to myfelf that Neck upon Nantuckett called Mafquetuck, or that Neck of Land called Nafhayte, the Neck (but one) northerly of Mafquetuck, ye aforefaid Sayle in anywife notwithftanding. And further, I ye faid Thomas Mayhew am to beare my Parte of the Charge of ye faid Purchafe abovenamed, and to hold one-twentieth Part of all Lands purchafed already, or fhall be hereafter purchafed upon ye faid Ifland, by ye aforef^d Purchafr^s or Heyres and Alllgnes forever. Briefly: It is thus; That I really fold all my Patent to ye aforefaid nine Men, and they are to pay mee, or whomfoever I fhall appoint them, ye Sume of Thirty Pounds in good Marchantable Pay in ye Maffachufetts, under wch Governm^t they now Inhabit, and 2 Beaver Hatts, and I am to beare a 20th Part of ye Charge of ye Purchase, and to have a 20th Part of all Lands and Priviledges; and to have wch of ye Necks abovef^d that I will myfelfe, paying for it; only ye Purchafers are to pay what ye Sachem Is to have for Mafquetuck, although I have ye other Neck.

And in Witnefs hereof, I have hereunto fett my Hand and Seale this fecond Day of July, fixteen hundred and fifty-nine, 1659.

Per me. THO: MAYHEW.

Witnefs
   JOHN SMYTH.
   EDWARD SCALE.

Deed of Tuckanucket Ifland.

[Deeds iii, 57, Secretary's Office.]

Recorded for Mr Coffin and Mr Macy aforefaid ye Day and Yeare Afore-written.

The tenth Day of October, one thoufand fix hundred fifty and nine; Thefe Prefents Witnefs, That I, Thomas Mayhew, of Martin's Vineyard, Merch^t. doe Give, Grant, Bargaine, and Sell, all my Right and Intereft in Tuckanuck Ifland, als Tuckanuckett, which I have had, or ought to have, by Vertue of Patent Right, purchafed of ye Lord Stirling's Agent and of Mr Richard Vines, Agent unto Sir Fferdhinando George, Knight, unto Triftram Coffin Sr. Peter Coffin, Triftram Coffin Junr. and James Coffin, to them and their Heyres forever, ffor and in confideracon of ye juft Sume of fix Pounds in Hand paid, and by mee Thomas Mayhew, received in full Satisfaction of ye aforefaid Patent Right, of ye aforefaid Ifland.

And in Witnefs hereof, I have fett my Hand and Seale.

Per me, THOMAS MAYHEW.

Witnefs hereunto,
   ROGER WHEELER.
   GEORGE WHEELER.

Deed of Wanockmamuck.

This witnesseth that I, Wanochmamack, chife sachem of Nantucket, hath sold unto Mr. Tristram Coffin and Thomas Macy, their heirs and assigns, that whole nack of land called by the Indians, Pacummohquah, being at the east end of Nantucket, for and in consideration of five pounds to be paid to me in English goods or otherwise to my content by the said Tristram Coffin aforesaid at convenient time as shall be demanded. Witness my hand or mark this 22 of June, 1662.

WANACKMAMAK.

Witness hereto:
PETER FOLGER & WAWINNESIT whose English name is AMOS.

Indian Deed of Nantucket.

[Deeds iii, 54, Secretary's Office.]

Recorded for Mr. Triftram Coffin and Mr. Thomas Macy, ye 29th of June, 1671 aforefaid.

Thefe Prefents Wittnefs, y^t I, Wanackmamack, Head Sachem of ye Ifland of Nantuckett, have Bargained and Sold, and doe by thefe Prefents Bargaine and Sell unto Triftram Coffin, Thomas Macy, Rich^d

Swayne, Thomas Bernard, John Swayne, Mr. Thomas Mayhew, Edward
Starbuck, Peter Coffin, James Coffin, Stephen Greenleafe, Triftram
Coffin Junr, Thomas Coleman, Robert Bernard, Chriftopher Huffey,
Robert Pike, John Smythe, and John Bifhop, thefe Iflands of *Nantuckett*,
namely, all ye Weft end of ye aforefd Ifland unto ye Pond comonly called
Waquittaquay, and from ye Head of that Pond to ye North fide of ye
Ifland *Manamoy*; Bounded by a Path from ye Head of ye Pond aforefaid
to *Manamoy*; as alfo a Neck at ye Eaft End of ye Ifland called *Poquo-
mock*, wth the Property thereof, and all ye Royaltyies, Priviledges, and
Immunityes thereto belonging, or whatfoever Right I ye aforefd Wan-
ackmak have, or have had in ye Same: That is, all ye Lands aforemenconed and likewife ye Winter ffeed of ye whole Ifland from ye End
of an Indyan Harveft untill Planting Time, or ye firft of May, from
Yeare to Yeare for ever; as likewife Liberty to make Ufe of Wood and
Timber on all Parts of ye Ifland; and likewife Halfe of the Meadows
and Marifhes on all Parts of ye Ifland, wthout or befide ye aforefd Tracts
of Land purchafed; And likewife ye ufe of ye other Halfe of ye Meadows
and Marif hes on all Parts of ye Ifland, wthout or befide ye aforefd Tracts
of Land purchafed; And likewife ye ufe of ye other Halfe of ye Meadows
and Marithes, as long as ye aforefaid Englifh their Heyres and Affignes
live on ye Ifland; And likewife I the aforefaid *Wanackmamack* doe fell
unto ye Englifh aforemenconed ye propriety of ye reft of ye Ifland belonging unto mee, for and in confideracon of ffourty Pounds already received
by mee or other by my Confent or Ordr. To Have and to Hold, ye
aforefd Tracts of Land wth ye Ppriety, Royalties, Immunityes, Prive-
leges and all Appertenances thereunto belonging to them ye aforef Pur-
chaf rs their Heyres and Affignes forever.
In Witnefs Whereof, I the aforefd Wanackmamack have hereunto fett
my Hand and Scale ye Day and Yeare above written.
                          The Signe of WANACK-MAMACK.
Signed, Sealed and Delivered in ye prfence of
     PETER FOULGER,
     ELEAZER FOULGER,
     DORCAS STARBUCK.

Indian Receipt for Land—Receipt of Wanackmanack.

[Nantucket Records, Old Book, Page 27.]

Received of Triftram Coffin, of Nantucket, the Juft fum of five
poun, which is part of the feven pound that was unpaid of the Twenty
pound Purchafe of Land, that was purchafed of Wanackmanack and
Neckanoofe, that is to fay, from Monomoy to Waquettaquage pond,
Nanahumack neck, and all from Wefco weftward to the Weft end of
Nantucket, I fay, Received by me, Wanackmamak, of Triftram Coffin,
five pounds Starling, the 18th 11 m, 1671.
                          the X mark of
                          WANACKMAMAK.

Witnefs hereunto:
     RICHARD GARDNER,
     ELEZER FOLGER.

Two Letters or Certificates from the Inhabitants of Nantucket.

[Deeds iii, 58, Secretary's Office, Albany.]

Recorded for ye aforefaid Mr. Coffin and Mr. Macy, 2 Lives on Certificates, from ye Inhabitants of Nantuckett, as followeth, vizt.

WHEREAS ye Honble Coll: Lovelace, Governour of New Yorke, gave forth his Summons for ye Inhabitants of ye Ifle of Nantuckett to make their Appearance before his Hono^r at New Yorke, either in their own Perfon or by their Agent, to fhew their Claymes in refpect to their Standing or Clayme of Intereft on ye aforefaid Ifland. Now wee whofe Names are underwritten having intrufted our ffather Triftram Coffin to make Anfwer for us, Wee doe Empower our ffather Triftram Coffin to act and doe for us wth ye Hon^d Govern^r Lovelace, foe far as is Juft and Reasonable, wth Regard to our Intereft, on ye Ifle of *Nantuckett* and *Tuckanuckett.*

Witnefs our Hands ye 2^d Day of ye fourth Month, fixteen hundred and feventy-one, 1671.

> JAMES COFFIN,
> NATHANIEL STARBUCK.
> JOHN COFFIN,
> STEPHEN COFFIN.

This is to Signify that ye Inhabitants of *Nantuckett* have chofen Mr. Thomas Macy their Agent to Treat wth ye Honble Coll: Lovelace concerning ye Affayres of ye Ifland, to Act for them in their Behalfe and Stead, and in all Confideracons to doe what is neceffary to be done in reference to ye Premifes, as if they themfelves were Perfonally prefent.

Witnefs their Hands, dated June 5th, 1671.

> EDWARD STARBUCK,
> PETER FFOULGER,
> JOHN ROLFE.

The Inhabitants aforef^d doe also in ye name of ye reft, defire Mr. Triftram Coffin to affift their aforef^d Agent what hee can in ye matter or Bufynefs concerning ye Ifland *Nantuckett.*

Propofals to ye Governor from ye Inhabitants of Nantuckett about settling that Government.

[Deeds iii, 59, Secretary's Office.]

Imprimis, Wee humbly propofe Liberty for ye Inhabitants to chufe annually a Man or Men to be Chiefe in ye Governm^t, and chofen or appointed by his Hono^r to Stand in place, conftantly invefted wth Power of Confirmacon by Oath or Engagem^t, or otherwife as his Hono^r fhall appoint, one to be Chiefe in ye Cor^t and to have Magiftraticall Power at all times wth regard to ye Peace and other neceffary Confideracons.

2ly. Wee take for granted y^t ye Lawes of England are Standard of Governm^t, foe farre as wee know them, and are fuitable to our Condicon; yet wee humbly propofe that ye Inhabitants may have Power to Conftitute fuch Law or Ord^{rs} as are neceffary and fuitable to o^r Condicon not repugnant to ye Lawes of England..

3ly. In point of carrying on ye Governm^t from Time to Time, wee are willing to joyne with o^r Neighbo^r Ifland ye Vineyard, to keep together one Cor^t every Yeare, one Yeare at o^r Ifland, ye next wth them, and

Power at Home to End all Cafes not exceeding 20 lb; And in all cafes
Liberty of Appeale to yᵉ Genᵉˡˡ Cᵒʳᵗ in all Actions above 40 lb. And in
all Actions amounting to yᵉ valine of 100 lb Liberty of Appeale to his
Highneffe his Cᵒʳᵗ at yᵉ Citty of New York; And in Capitall Cafes, or
fuch Mattʳˢ as concerne Life, Limbe, or Banifhmᵗ. All fuch cases to be
tryed at New Yorke.

4. And feeling yᵉ Indyans are numerous among us. Wee propofe
that oʳ Governmᵗ may Extend to them, and Power to Summon them to
our Cᵒʳᵗˢ wᵗʰ respect to Mattʳˢ of Trefpafs Debt, and other Mifcarriages,
and to Try and Judge them according to Lawes, when publifhed amongft
them.

And Laftly, fome Military Power committed to us, refpecting our
Defence, either in refpect of Indyans or Strangʳˢ invadeing, &c.

The Anfwer to yᵉ Nantucket Propofals.

[Deeds iii, 60, Secretary's Office.]

At a Councell held at Forte James in New York, yᵉ 28ᵗʰ day of June in
yᵉ 23ᵈ Yeare of his Matⁱᵉˢ Reigne, Annoᵒ Dom. 1671

In Anfwer to yᵉ Propofalls Delivered in by Mr. Coffin and Mr. Macy
on yᵉ behalf of themfelves and yᵉ reft of yᵉ Inhabitants upon yᵉ Ifland
Nantuckett: The Governoʳ and Councell doe give their Refolucons as
followeth, viᵗ.

Imprimis, As to yᵉ firft Branch in their Propofalls, It is thought fitt
yᵗ yᵉ Inhabitants doe annually recomend two Perfons to the Governoʳ,
out of wᶜʰ hee will Nominate one to be yᵉ Chiefe Magiftrate upon that
Ifland, and yᵉ Ifland of Tuckanuckett near adjacent for yᵉ Yeare enfue-
ing: who fhall by Commiffion bee Invefted with Power accordingly.

That yᵉ Time when fuch a Magiftrate fhall Enter into his Employmᵗ
after yᵉ Expiracon of this firft Yeare, fhall Commence upon yᵉ 13ᵗʰ day
of October, being his Royall Highnefs his Birthday, to continue for yᵉ
Space of one whole Yeare, and that they Returne yᵉ Names of yᵉ two
Perfons they fhall recommend three months before that Time to yᵉ Governoʳ.

That yᵉ Inhabitⁱˢ have Power by a Major Vote annually to Elect and
Chufe their inferior Officers, both Civill and Military: That is to fay, yᵉ
Affiftants, Conftables, and other Inferior Officers, for yᵉ Civill Governmᵗ,
and fuch inferior Officeʳˢ for yᵉ Military as fhall be thought needfull.

2ʸ. The fecond Propofall is allowed of: That they fhall have Liberty to make peculiar Lawes and Ordʳˢ at their Genᵉˡˡ Cᵒʳᵗ for the well
Governmᵗ of yᵉ Inhabitⁱˢ yᵉ wᶜʰ fhall bee in force amongft them for one
whole Yeare; Dureing wᶜʰ Time if noe Inconvenience doe appeare
therein, They are to Tranfmitt the faid Lawes or Ordʳˢ to yᵉ Governoʳ
for his Confirmacon. Howevʳ, They are (as neare as may bee) to con-
forme themfelves to yᵉ Lawes of England, and to be very Cautions they
doe not Act in any way repugnant to them.

3ˡʸ. To yᵉ 3ᵈ, It is Granted, That they joyne wᵗʰ their Neighbors of
Martin's Vineyard in keeping a Genᵉˡˡ Cᵒʳᵗ between them once a Yeare,
yᵉ fᵈ Cᵒʳᵗ to be held one Yeare in one Ifland, and yᵉ next in yᵉ other,
where yᵉ Chiefe Magiftrate in each Ifland where the Cᵒʳᵗ fhall be held,
is to prefide, and to Sitt in their refpective Cᵒʳᵗˢ as Prefidt, but withall
That upon all occafions hee Confuel and Advize wᵗʰ yᵉ Chiefe Magiftrate
of yᵉ other Ifland.

That ye faid Genꝛll Cort fhall confift of ye two Chiefe Magiftrates of both Iflands, and ye foure Affiftants, where ye Prefidt fhall have a Cafting Voyce; for ye Time of their Meeting, That it bee left to themfelves to Agree upon ye moft convenient Seafon of ye Yeare.

That in their Private Corts at Home, weh are to be held by ye Chiefe Magiftrate and two Affiftts where ye Chiefe Magiftrate fhall have but a fingle Voyce, They fhall have Power finally to determine and decide all Cafes not exceeding ye Vallue of 5 lb. wthout Appeale, but in any Sume above that Vallue, They have Liberty of Appeale to their Genꝛll Cort who may determine abfolutely any Cafe under 50 lb. without Appeale, but if it fhall exceed that Sume, ye Party aggrieved may have Recourfe by way of Appeale to ye Genꝛll Cort of Affizes, held in New Yorke.

And as to Criminal Cafes, That they have Power both at their Private Corts at Home, as well as at ye Genꝛll Cort, to inflict Punifhmt on Offendꝛ foe farre as Whipping, Stocks, and Pilloring, or other Publick Shame. But if ye Crime happen to bee of a higher nature, where Life, Limbe, or Banifhment are concerned, That fuch Mattꝛ be Tranfmitted to ye Genꝛll Cort of Affizes likewife.

4. In Anfwr to ye 4th, It is left to themfelves to Ordr thofe Affayres about ye Indyans, and to Act therein according to their beft diferetions, foe farr as Life is not concerned; Wherein they are also to have Recourfe to New Yorke, but that they bee carefull to ufe fuch moderacon amongft them, That they bee not exafperated, but by Degrees may be brought to be conformable to ye Lawes; To wch End, They are to Nominate and appoint Conftables amongft them who may have Staves wth ye Kings Armes upon them, the better to keep their People in Awe and good Ordr, as is practized wth good fuccefs amongft ye Indyans at ye Eaft end of Long Ifland.

To ye Laft, That they returne a Lyft of ye Inhabitants, as alfo ye Names of two Perfons amongft them; out of whom ye Governor will appoint one to bee their Chiefe Military Officer, That they may be in ye better capacity to Defend themfelves againft their Enemyes, whether Indyans or others.

Nantucket Affayres.

[Deeds iii, 85, Secretary's Office.]

Additionall Inftructions and Directions for the Government of the Ifland Nantuckett, fent by Mr. Richard and Capt. Jno. Gardner, Aprill ye 18th, 1673.

Imprimis, That in regard ye Towne upon ye Ifland of *Nantuckett* is not known by any peculiar or particular Name, It fhall from henceforth bee called and diftinguifhed in all Deeds, Records and Writings by the Name of the Town of *Sherborne* upon the Ifland *Nantuckett*.

That all Ancient and Obfolete Deeds, Grants, Writings, or Conveyances of Lands upon the faid Ifland, fhall bee efteemed of noe fforce or Validity, but the Records of everyones Clayme or Intereft fhall beare Date from the firft Divulging of the Patent granted to the Inhabitants by Authority of his Royall Highneffe, and foe forward, but not before the Date thereof.

That the Time of Election of the Chiefe Magiftrate, and other Civill Officers, bee and continue according to the Directions and Inftructions already given, but in regard of the Diftance of the Place, and ye uncer-

A3

tainty of Conveyance betwixt that and this Place, yͤ Chiefe Magistrate, and all the Civill Officers fhall continue in their Employmtˢ untill the Returne of the Governorˢ Choice and Approbacon of a new Magistrate bee fent unto them, which is to be with the first convenient Opportunity.

That in cafe of Mortality, if it fhall pleafe God, the Chiefe Magistrate fhall dye before yͤ Expiration of his Employment, the Affiftants for the Time being fhall manage and carry on yͤ Affayres of the Public untill the Time of the new Election, and yͤ Governorˢ Returne and Approbation of a new Magiftrate in his Stead.

That the Chiefe Military Officer fhall continue in his Employmt during the Governorˢ Pleafure, and that he have Power to appoint fuch Perfons for inferior Officers as he fhall judge moft fitt and capable.

That in Cafe of the Death of the Chiefe Military Officer during the Time of his Employment, that then the Inhabitantˢ doe forthwith make Choice of two Perfons, and returne their Names unto the Governour, who will appoint one of them to bee the Officer in his Stead.

That in regard to yͤ Generall Coͬᵗ to bee held in yͤ Ifland *Nantuckett* or *Martin's Vineyard* is but once in yͤ Yeare, where all Caufes or Actions are tryable without Apeale to yͤ Sume of fifty Pounds. Liberty bee granted to try all Actions of Debt or Trefpass at their ordinary Courts to the value of ten Pounds without Appeale, unlefs upon Occafion of Error in yͤ Proceeding there bee Caufe of Complaint from yͤ ordinary Court unto the Generall Court, or from the Genͤˡˡ Court to the Court of Affizeˢ.

That what is granted in the Generall Patent to the Inhabitantˢ, freeholders, of the Ifland *Nantuckett* is to bee underftood, unto them alone who live upon the Place and make Improvemᵗ thereof, or fuch others who having Pretences of Intereft fhall come to Inhabitt there.

Given under my Hand at Fort James, in New York the Day and Yeare afore written; and in yͤ 25th Yeare of his Matˡⁱᵉˢ Reigne.

Decifion of a Court of Admiralty held at Nantucket.

[New York Colonial MSS, xxix, Sec. Office.]

At a Court of Admiralty, held at the Ifland of Nantuckett yͤ twenty-eighth day of Auguft, by his Matⁱᵉˢ Athority, in the thirty-fecond Yeare of the Reiagne of our Sovereigne Lord King Charles the Second, and in the Yeare of our Lord on thoufand fix hundred and eighty.

Prefent, Captⁿ Cefar Knapton,
 Captⁿ Richard Hall,
 Mr John Weft,
 Capᵗ John Gardner, Magiftrate.

Mr. Triftram Coffin, late Magiftrate, being called to give an Accoumpt of what was faued out of the Rack of a French Ship, caft away on this Ifland by fome of Capt. Bernard Lamoyn's Men, about the latter Part of the Yeare feventy-eight, declared he had formerly giuen an Accoumpt, which being produced and read, it appeared that thare ware faued out of the faid Rack two thoufaud and fixteen Hydes, which he confefteth are difpofed of by his Order, Alowance and Aprobation, and by Information giuen, we valleu at fouer Shillings per Hyde, which amounts toe fouer hundred and three Pounds fouer Shillings; and alfo one Cable and a Pece, likewife fold by the faid Triftram Coffin at forty fouer Pounds; and one Sayle at fix Pounds ten Shillings; and two Pecls of Hafers at eleuen Pounds, and an Ancker at thirteen Pounds; which in all amounts toe fouer hundred feventy-feuen Pounds fourteen Shillings, for which no Claime hath bin made according to Law.

This Court tharefore, taking into Confideration the Allowance of Salvage of faid Goods, and vnderftanding the Difeculty and Hardfhip the Sauers endured, doe alow on fifth Part thareof for Salvage, according to Law, which amounts toe ninety-five Pounds ten Shillings And for what was difburfed by the faid Triftram Coffin on Accompt of fome Duch Prifïoners left one the Ifland, and what was paid by him to William Worth, for his Wound, forty Pound one Shilling. In all, on hundred thirty-five Pounds eleauen Shillings; which being deducted out of the faid Sum of fower hundred feventy feauen Pounds fourteen Shillings. They doe adjudge and determine that the faid Coffin doe make Payment and Sattisfaction toe the Gouernor or his Order, on Accompt of his Royall Highnefs to whom by Law it doth appertain the Remainder of of the faid Sum, being three hundred forty-three Pounds ten Shillings. And as for what Guns or Rigeing or other Things that are vndifpofed of, toe be apprifed and Salvage to be alowed as aboue, and to be fent to New York for his Royall Highnefe vfe. the Salvage toe be lickwife paid by the faid Coffin, to be deduckted out of the three hundred fourty-three Pounds ten Shillings. They Court lickewife declare thare Opinion that the faid Coffin's Actings Proceedings in difpofing of the faid Goods, are contrary to Law.

By Order of the Court, &c.

WILLIAM WORTH, Clerk.

Triftram Coffin to Sir Edmond Andros.

[New York Colonial MSS, xxix, Sec. Office.]

To the Right Honrabell Ser Edmund Andros, Knight, Signeur of Safmaryoc, Lieut. Generall vnder his Royall Hynes James Duke of York and Albany, and Gouernor Generall of all his Royall Hynes Territorys in America. Thefe Prefent. [External Scale ftamped with a Pine Tree Shilling.]

Nantuckett, 30th of Auguft, 1680.

Right Honerabell Sir:

My humbell Service prefented vnto your Excellencye humblie fhewing my hartie Sorow yt I fhould in any way giue your Exelency juft occafion of Offence, as I now plainly fee, in actinge contrary to the Law, as I am conuinced I did, throw Ignorance in regard of not beinge acquainted with the maretime Lawes, and yet I humblie intreat your Exelency to confider yt in on Refpect my weeacknefs I hope may bee a littell born with : for I did tender diuerfe Perfons the on halfe to faue the other halfe, and I could not get any to doe it: and for the Hides I could not get any to goe but for to tacke all for their Labor, becaufe it was judged by many yt the weare not worth the fauing ; fo I was nefefetated to doe as I did or elfe the had bin quite loft. Tharefore I humblye intreat your Excelency not to think yt I did it for any bye Refpects or felfe Ends; for I doe affure your Excelency yt theare was not any on Perfon yt did indent with me for any on Shillinge Proffit, only I did tell foure of them yt if I fhould bee by any cal'd to accot, the fhould bee accountabell to me. But now the will not owne it and I can not proue it, fo I by Law am cauft to beare all, only my hop is yt your Excelency will bee pleafed out of your Leniency and Fauor to me to except of int Money, and Bill is fent for the anfweringe of the Judgment of the Court; for had not my Sonn, James Coffyn borrowed Money and ingaged for the reft of my Bill, I could not have done it, but I muft have gone to Prifon. Now I humblye intreat your Excelency to heare my louinge Nighbor, Capt John Gardner, in my behaife, and wth your Exelency fhall bee pleafed to order Concerning the Cafe, I fhall thankfulye except, knowing your Excelency to be a compaffionate, merceyfull Man. And I hop I fhall for Time to com . . . . . to be more wifer and doe kept your Excelency's humbell Saruant whylft I liue to my Power.

TRISTRAM COFFYN.

A Discharge to Mr. Tristram Coffin from the Judgment of the Court of Admiralty Compounded.

[Warrants, Orders, Paffes, &c., xxii 1-2, 9, Secretary's Office.]

By the Governor:

These are to Certifie that I doe approve and allow of the Compofition and Agreem[t] made between Capt. Cæfar Knapton, Capt. Richard Hall, Capt. John Gardner, and Mr. John Weft, who were authorized to make Enquiry ab[t] the Wreck of a French fhip caft away on the Ifland of Nantuckett in one thoufand fix hundred feventy and eight, and Mr. Triftram Coffin, then Chiefe Magiftrate of the faid Ifland, concerning the fame, for the fume of one hundred and fifty Pound, halfe of which is payd; and on paym[t] of the other halfe, fecured by his Sonn's Obligacon, I doe accept the fame in full Satisfaction and hereby acquitt and difcharge the faid Truftram Coffin from the Judgm[t] giuen againft him in the Court of Admiralty, on Account of faid Wreck.

Given under my Hand in New Yorke, the fixth Day of November, 1680.

E. A.

DESCENDANTS OF TRISTRAM AND DIONIS.

HON. PETER COFFIN, eldest child of Tristram and Dionis, was born at Brixton, County of Devon, England, in 1631. He married Abigail, daughter of Edward and Katherine Starbuck, of Dover, N. H., afterwards of Nantucket. He was one of the original purchasers of Nantucket, and tradition says the wealthiest of them, owning large mill property. He was a merchant at Dover before the purchase, and subsequently lived at Nantucket, but only for a short time to be considered as domiciled there. He was made freeman in 1666, at Dover; a Lieutenant in 1675, on service in King Philip's Indian war; a Representative in the Legislative branch in 1672–3 and again in 1679. In 1690 he removed to Exeter, N. H. From 1692 to 1714 he was at different times associate justice and chief justice of the Supreme Court of New Hampshire, and a member of the Governor's Council. He died at Exeter, March 21, 1715, but most of his life was passed at Dover.

In administering the functions of his several official positions there arose many questions of grave importance, and one which, as a judge, has been handed down as a specimen of religious persecution. The Reverend Joshua Moodey had gathered a church at Portsmouth, N. H., and distinguished himself as an independent preacher. One of his parishioners had been interested in seizing and carrying out of the harbor a Scotch ketch [a heavy ship] and upon trial had sworn falsely, but the Lieutenant Governor, Cranfield, at the head of the province, had adjusted the matter with the offender and discharged him. But pastor Moodey took it up and called church meetings upon the subject, which irritated Gov. Cranfield, and Moodey was indicted under the uniformity act in 1684, and imprisoned thirteen weeks, and then dismissed with the charge to preach no more under penalty. He was advised to leave Portsmouth and preached in the old church at Boston for a time afterward. And in 1683, he returned to Portsmouth and commenced preaching again, when he was again arrested. Peter Coffin was one of the judges which convicted him, and in his own language Moodey thus pours out his vials of wrath as copied from his records and published in Mass. Hist. Society's Coll., vol. x, p. 44, 1809:

"The Judge of the court was [captain of the fort] Walter Barefoot, the justices Mr. Fryer, Peter Coffin, Thomas Edgerly, Henry Green, and Henry Robey. Overnight, four of the six dissented from his imprisonment; but, before next morning, Peter Coffin, being hectored by Cranfield, drew off Robey and Green. Only Mr. Fryer and Edgerly refused to consent, but by the major part he was committed. Not long after, Green repented and made his acknowledgment to the pastor, who frankly forgave him. Robey was excommunicated out of Hampton church for a common drunkard, and died excommunicate, and was by his friends thrown into a hole, near his house, for fear of an arrest of his carcase. Barefoot fell into a languishing distemper, whereof he died. Coffin was taken by the Indians and his house and mills burnt, himself not slain but dismissed. The Lord give him repentance, though no sign of it have appeared. Psalm lx. 16."

His election as one of the magistrates of Nantucket under a period of great excitement has been before alluded to. The early records of Nantucket are frequently devoted to transactions of Peter Coffin, in the purchase and sale of land, and of gifts and grants to his children, and would be interesting to reproduce in a larger work. The lumber for his son Jethro's house, now the oldest house standing on Nantucket, was the product of one of his mills. His children:

Abigail, b. Oct. 20, 1657; m. Dec. 16, 1673, Daniel Davidson, of Ipswich, afterwards of Newbury.
Peter, Jr., b. Aug. 20, 1660; m. Aug. 15, 1682, Elizabeth, d. of Nathaniel and Mary Starbuck; d. in Nantucket in 1699.
Jethro, b. Sept. 16, 1663; m. Mary, d. of Hon. John and Priscilla Gardner; d. in 1726.
Tristram, b. Jan. 18, 1665; m. Deborah Colcord.
Robert, b. in 1667; m. Joanna, daughter of Hon. John Gilman, of Exeter, N. H., widow of Henry Dyer; d. May 19, 1710. No issue.
Edward, b. Feb. 20, 1669; m. Anna, d. of Hon. John and Priscilla Gardner.
Judith, b. Feb. 4, 1672.
Parnell, died in infancy.
Elizabeth, born Jan. 27, 1680; m. June 5, 1698, Col. John Gilman, of Exeter, N. H.; d. July 4, 1720.
Eliphalet, died single.

TRISTRAM COFFIN, JR., second child, was born in England, in 1632. He married in Newbury, Mass., March 2, 1652, Judith Somerby, widow of Henry, and daughter of Edmund and Sarah Greenleaf. She was born in 1625, and died in Newbury, Dec. 15, 1705. He was made freeman April 29, 1668, and died in Newbury, Feb. 4, 1704, aged 72, leaving 177 descendants. He was a merchant tailor, and filled many positions of trust and honor in Newbury. The early records of Newbury bear evidence of his identity with the interests of that town. In the severe ecclesiastical contest concerning Rev. Thomas Parker, of Newbury, Tristram Coffin, Jr., bore a conspicuous part in the interest of Mr. Parker, of whose first church of Newbury he was deacon for twenty years. He built, about 1654, according to the historian of Newbury, the old Coffin mansion, which has remained in the family to the present day, one of the ninth generation born under its ample roof, Miss Anna L. Coffin, now occupying it. Mr. Thomas Coffin Amory, however, says that it was built in 1649, by Henry Somerby, whose widow, it will be remembered, Tristram Coffin, Jr., married. It is one of the few old houses left, and is built around a vast chimney stack with spacious fire-places, with windows large and small opening in pleasant surprises, some on closets and some on staircases, and with walls that, when stripped of their papering not many years ago for the purpose of repapering, were found to display such elegant landscape frescoes with artistic designs of figures and foliage as were wont to decorate fine residences in the days of the Stuarts. It is a matter of tradition that Tristram Coffyn, senior, lived in this old mansion a short time before his final removal to Nantucket.

Two monuments in the grave yard of the first parish of Newbury bear these several inscriptions :

" To the memory of Tristram Coffin, Esq., who having served the first church of Newbury in the office of a deacon 20 years died Feb. 4, 1703-4 aged 72 years.

> " On earth he purchased a good degree
> Great boldness in the faith and liberty
> And now possesses immortality."

" To the memory of Mrs. Judith, late virtuous wife of Deac. Tristram Coffin, Esq., who, having lived to see 177 of her children and children's children to the 3d generation, died Dec. 15, 1705, aged 80.

> " Grave, sober, faithful, fruitful vine was she,
> A rare example of true piety.
> Widow'd awhile she wayted wisht-for rest,
> With her dear husband in her Saviours breast."

Tristram Junior's children :

Judith, b. in Newbury, Mass., Dec. 4, 1653; m. John Sanborn, of Hampton, N. H., Nov. 19, 1674.
Deborah, b. in Newbury, Nov. 10, 1655; m. Joseph Knight, Oct. 31, 1677.
Mary, b. in Newbury, Nov. 12, 1557; m. Joseph Little, Oct. 31, 1677.
James, b. in Newbury, April 22, 1659; m. Florence Hooke, Nov. 16, 1685.
John, b. in Newbury, Sept. 8, 1660; d. there May 13, 1677.
Lydia, b. in Newbury, April 22, 1662; m. 1st, Moses Little; 2d, March 18, 1695, John Pike.
Enoch, b. in Newbury, Jan. 21, 1663; d. there Nov. 12, 1675.
Stephen, b. in Newbury, Aug. 18, 1664; m. Sarah Atkinson, Oct. 8, 1685; d. Aug. 31, 1725.

Peter, b. in Newbury, July 27, 1667; m. Apphia Dole; d. in Gloucester, (?) Jan. 19, 1746.
Nathaniel, Hon., b. in Newbury, March 22, 1669; m. Sarah Dole, March 29, 1693; d. Feb. 20, 1748-9.

ELIZABETH COFFIN, third child, was born in England, about 1634-5. She married, in Newbury, Nov. 13, 1651, Capt. Stephen Greenleaf, son of Edmund. She died at Newbury, Nov. 19, 1678. He died Dec. 1, 1690. From this family have descended the Greenleafs of New England, among whom have been many ripe scholars, eminent as jurists, teachers and divines. Their children were:

Stephen Greenleaf, b. Aug. 15, 1652; m. Oct. 23, 1676, Elizabeth Gerrish, dau. of William.
Sarah Greenleaf, b. Oct. 29, 1655; m. June 7, 1677, Richard Dole, of Newbury, son of Richard.
Daniel Greenleaf, b. Feb. 17, 1658.
Elizabeth Greenleaf, b. April 9, 1660; m. 1677, Thomas Noyes, son of James.
John Greenleaf, b. June 21, 1662; m. Oct. 12, 1685, Elizabeth Hills.
Samuel Greenleaf, b. Oct. 30, 1665; m. March 1, 1689, Sarah Kent, dau. of John.
Tristram Greenleaf, b. Feb. 11, 1668; m. Nov. 12, 1689, Margaret Piper.
Edmund Greenleaf, b. May 10, 1670; m. July 2, 1691, Abigail Somerby, dau. of Abiel.
Judith Greenleaf, b. Oct. 13, 1673; d. Sept. 30, 1690.
Mary Greenleaf, b. Dec. 6, 1676; m. Joshua Moody, son of Caleb.

HON. JAMES COFFIN, the fourth child, was born in England, Aug. 12, 1640. He married, Dec. 3, 1663, Mary, daughter of John and Abigail Severance, of Salisbury, Mass.; and died at Nantucket, July 28, 1720, aged 80 years. He came to Nantucket with the first settlers, but subsequently removed to Dover, N. H., where he resided in 1668, being a member of the church there in 1671, and the same year, May 31, he was there made freeman. Soon after this date, however, he returned to Nantucket and resided there until his death. He filled several important public offices at Nantucket, among them Judge of the Probate Court. The first records of the Probate Office are under his administration. He was the father of fourteen children, all of whom, except two, grew to maturity and married. From him have descended, perhaps, the most remarkable representatives of the Coffin family, as doubtless the most numerous and generally scattered. This branch furnished the families that remained loyal to Great Britain in the American Revolution, and General John Coffin, as well as his brother, Admiral Sir Isaac Coffin, rendered valiant service against the Colonies, for which they received in time their rewards, two sons of Gen. John now holding Admiral's commissions in the Royal Navy, one aged 88 and the other 84 years, both hale and hearty when last heard from. The most distinguished

woman which America has produced, Lucretia Mott, was also descended
from this line, her father, Thomas Coffin, being the 17th child of Benjamin, and not the youngest, either. The children of James are:

Mary, b. in Nantucket, April 18, 1665; married first, Richard Pinkham,
of Portsmouth, N. H., who came from the Isle of Wight, and died in
Nantucket in 1718; second, James, son of Richard and Sarah Gardner;
d. in Nantucket, Feb. 1, 1741.
James, Jr., b. probably in Dover, N. H.; m., first, Love, dau. of Richard
and Sarah Gardner; second, Ruth, dau. of John and Priscilla Gardner;
d. in Nantucket, Oct. 2, 1741.
Nathaniel, b. in Dover, 1671; m. Aug. 17, 1692, Damaris, dau. of Wm.
Gayer; d. Aug. 29, 1721.
John, b. in Nantucket; m. Hope Gardner, dau. of Richard; d. there July
1, 1747.
Dinah, b. in Nantucket; m. Nov. 20, 1690, Nathaniel Starbuck, Jr.; d.
there Aug. 1, 1750.
Deborah, b. in Nantucket; m. Oct. 10, 1695, George Bunker, son of
Wm.; d. there Oct. 8, 1767.
Ebenezer, b. in Nantucket, March 30, 1678; m. Dec. 12, 1700, Eleanor,
dau. of Nathaniel Barnard; died there Oct. 17, 1730.
Joseph, b. in Nantucket, Feb. 4, 1680; m. Bethia, dau. of John Macy; d.
there July 14, 1719.
Elizabeth, b. in Nantucket; m., first, Jonathan, son of Wm. and Mary
Bunker; second, Thomas Clark; d. there, March 30, 1769.
Benjamin, b. in Nantucket, Aug. 28, 1683; lost overboard between Nan-
tucket and Martha's Vineyard.
Ruth, b. in Nantucket; m. Joseph, son of Richard and Mary Gardner; d.
there, May 28, 1748.
Abigail, b. in Nantucket; m. Nathaniel, son of Richard and Sarah Gard-
ner; d. there March 15, 1709, and was the first person buried in Gard-
ner's burial ground.
Experience, b. in Nantucket and died young.
Jonathan, b. in Nantucket, August 28, 1692; m. Hephzibah, dau. of Ebenezer Harker; d. there Feb. 5, 1773.

JOHN COFFIN, fifth child, was born in England, and died in Haverhill, Mass., Oct. 30, 1642, in infancy.

DEBORAH COFFIN, sixth child, was born in Haverhill, Nov. 16, 1642,
and died there, Dec. 8, 1642, in infancy.

MARY COFFIN, seventh child, was born in Haverhill, Feb. 20, 1645.
She was married at the age of 17, to Nathaniel, son of Edward and
Katherine (Reynolds) Starbuck; and died at Nantucket, Nov. 13, 1717.
He died at Nantucket, the 2d day of the 2d month, 1719. Her eldest
child, Mary Starbuck, born March 30, 1663, was the first white child
born upon the island. From this family all of the Starbucks of
America are descended. She was a most extraordinary woman, participating in the practical duties and responsibilities of public gath-
erings and town meetings, on which occasions her words were always
listened to with marked respect. The genius of whatever attaches to
the Equal Rights for Woman movement of the present day, in every

true and proper sense, she anticipated by two centuries, and reduced to practice, without neglecting her domestic relations. She was consulted upon all matters of public importance, because her judgment was superior, and she was universally acknowledged to be a great woman. It was not that her husband, Nathaniel Starbuck, was a man of inferior mould, that she gained such prominence, for he was a man of good ability; but because of her pre-eminent qualifications that she acquired so good a reputation, whereby her husband's qualifications were apparently lessened. In the language of John Richardson, an early preacher, "The islanders esteemed her as a Judge among them, for little of moment was done without her." In the town meetings which she was accustomed to attend, she took an active part in the debates, usually commencing her address with "My husband thinks" so and so; or "My husband and I, having considered the subject, think" so and so. From every source of information, as also from tradition, there is abundant evidence that she was possessed of sound judgment, clear understanding, and an elegant way of expressing herself perfectly easy and natural to her. In 1701, at the age of 56, she became interested in the religious faith of the Quakers or Friends, and took the spiritual concerns of the whole island under her special superintendence. She held meetings at her own 'house which are often alluded to by visiting Friends who have written concerning the island's early religious history, wrote the quarterly epistles, and preached in a most eloquent and impressive manner; and, withal, was as distinguished in her domestic economy as she was celebrated as a preacher. Of this department John Richardson, who preached at her house, wrote, "The order of the house was such in all the parts thereof, as I had not seen the like before; the large and bright-rubbed room was set with suitable seats or chairs for a meeting, so that I did not see anything wanting according to place, but something to stand on, for I was not free to set my feet upon the fine cane chair, lest I should break it." Enough might be written concerning her to make an entertaining volume by itself, which may some time be attempted. Her children:

Mary Starbuck, b. March 30, 1663; m. James Gardner, son of Richard; d. 1696.
Elizabeth Starbuck, b. Sept. 9, 1665; m., first, Peter Coffin, Jr., son of Peter and Abigail (Starbuck) Coffin; second, Nathaniel Barnard, Jr., son of Nathaniel.
Nathaniel Starbuck, Jr., b. Aug. 9, 1668; m. Nov. 20, 1690, Dinah, daughter of James and Mary (Severance) Coffin; d. at Nantucket Jan. 29, 1753.
Jethro Starbuck, b. Dec. 14, 1671; m. Dec. 6, 1694, Dorcas, dau. of William and Dorcas (Starbuck) Gayer; d. Aug. 12, 1770.
Barnabus Starbuck, b. 1673; d. 9th mo., 21, 1732, unmarried.
Eunice Starbuck, b. April 11, 1674; m. George, son of John Gardner; d. 12th of 2d mo., 1766.

Priscilla Starbuck, b. 1676; m. John, son of John Coleman; d. March
14, 1762.
Hephzibah Starbuck, b. April 2, 1680; m. Thomas Hathaway of Dart-
mouth; d. 7th of 2d mo., 1740.
Ann, died single.
Paul, died single.

LIEUT. JOHN COFFIN, eighth child (a former John having died),
was born at Haverhill, Oct. 30, 1647. He married Deborah, daughter of
Joseph and Sarah Austin; and died at Edgartown, Mass., Sept. 5, 1711.
From him the Martha's Vineyard Coffins are descended. He removed to
Edgartown after his father's death, about 1682-3. He was elected to some
minor offices in Nantucket, and was at Edgartown commissioned a Lieutenant of Militia. He had eleven children, among them Enoch, who was
chief judge for Dukes County, and who had ten children, all of whom
lived to the age of rising 70 years, and six of the ten to above 80, and
two of them to 90, the most remarkable instance of family longevity yet
discovered. His children in order were:

Lydia, b. in Nantucket, June 1, 1669; m., first, John Logan; second,
John Draper; third, Thomas Thaxter of Hingham.
Peter, b. in Nantucket, Aug. 5, 1671; m., first, Christian Condy; second,
Hope, dau. of Joseph and Bethiah (Macy) Gardner; d. there Oct. 27,
1749.
John, Jr., b. in Nantucket, Feb. 10, 1673.
Love, b. in Nantucket, April 23, 1676; died single.
Enoch, b. in Nantucket, 1678; m. Beulah Eddy, about 1700; d. in Edgar-
town in 1761.
Samuel, b. in Nantucket; m. Miriam Gardner, dau. of Richard, Jr., 1705;
d. Feb. 22, 1764.
Hannah, b. in Nantucket; m. Benjamin Gardner, son of Richard, Jr.; d.
Jan. 28, 1768.
Tristram, b. in Nantucket; m. Mary Bunker, dau. of William, 1714; d.
Jan. 29, 1763.
Deborah, b. in Nantucket; m. June 18, 1718, Thomas Macy, son of John;
d. Sept. 23, 1760.
Elizabeth, b. in Nantucket; died single.
Benjamin, b. 8 mo., 23, 1683.

STEPHEN COFFIN, the youngest child, was born at Newbury, Mass.,
May 10, 1652, and was about 8 years old when his father removed to Nantucket. He married Mary, dau. of George and Jane (Godfrey) Bunker
about 1668-9, and died at Nantucket, Nov. 14, 1734. For him, to a considerable extent, Tristram reversed the old English law of leaving to the eldest
son his lands and estates and gave them to his youngest son. Stephen
appears to have remained upon his father's estate, and succeeded to the
management of the farm and general business cares, and by agreement
was to be helpful to his father and mother in their old age. He had ten
children, viz:

Daniel, b. at Nantucket; d. 4 mo., 1724—lost at sea.
Dionis, b. at Nantucket Sept. 21, 1671; m. Jacob Norton.
Peter, b. at Nantucket Nov. 14, 1673; m. in Boston.
Stephen, Jr., b. at Nantucket Feb. 20, 1675; m. 1693, Experience Look, dau. of Thomas.
Judith, b. at Nantucket; m., first, Peter Folger, son of Elezer; second, Nathaniel Barnard, son of Nathaniel; third, Stephen Wilcox; d. Dec. 2, 1760.
Susanna, b. at Nantucket; m. Peleg Bunker, son of William; d. June 11, 1740.
Mehitable, b. at Nantucket; m. Armstrong Smith.
Anna, b. at Nantucket; m. Solomon Gardner, son of Richard, 2d; d. April 22, 1740.
Hephzibah, b. at Nantucket; m. Samuel Gardner.
Paul, b. at Nantucket April 15, 1695; m. Mary Allen, dau. of Edward; d. April, 1729.

BIOGRAPHIES AND ANECDOTES OF DESCENDANTS.

The biographical and anecdotical feature of this publication is necessarily abridged on account of insufficient time to properly arrange and print before the first reunion of Tristram's descendants at Nantucket, August 16, 17, and 18, 1881. As many of his descendants have achieved fame and gained a just celebrity, it becomes a matter of extreme delicacy to select from among so many the few that space will permit to be noticed in this work. Those given, however, are but a fair representation of the many that might be, and which it is hoped some time will be, added to the biographies of Tristram Coffyn's descendants.

GEN. JOHN COFFIN, of St. John's New Brunswick, was an elder brother of Sir Isaac. He distinguished himself as a general in the English army against the colonies; and subsequently took up his residence at St. John's, N. B. In the war of 1812, he again took up arms in defence of his country, having always remained loyal to Great Britain. At the close of the Revolution he married Annie, daughter of William Matthews, of St. John's Island, South Carolina. Washington Irving in his life of Washington, states that the advance on Eutaw by Gen. Greene, supported by Col. William Washington, was averted by Major John Coffin, with 150 infantry and 50 cavalry. He was born at Boston, Mass., in 1756, and died at his residence in King's Co., New Brunswick, on the 2th of May, 1838, aged 82 years. His whole career was that of a vigorous, conscientious man of great ability.

ADMIRAL SIR ISAAC COFFIN, Baronet, was of the fifth generation from Tristram and descended as follows: Tristram[1], James[2], Nathaniel[3], William[4], Nathaniel[5], who married Elizabeth, daughter of Henry Barnes, of Boston. He was the fourth son, and was born at Boston, Mass., May 16, 1759. Entering the English Navy in 1773, he was commissioned a Lieutenant, 1778; Captain, 1781; Rear Admiral of the White Squadron, 1804; Baronet, and also granted a Coat of Arms the same year; Vice-Admiral, 1808; and in 1817 Admiral. He died at Cheltenham, England, in 1839, aged 80 years, without issue.

He was awarded an estate by the Government of England, known as the Magdelen Islands, at the mouth of the St. Lawrence River, about the time he was created a Baronet. He was a personal friend of the Duke of Clarence, who, when he became William IV., continued to show him favor. When it became necessary, in 1832, to swamp the House of Lords, by creating new Peers in order to pass the Reform Bill, the name of Sir Isaac was upon the King's list. He desired to make him Earl of Magdelen, but the Ministers objected, on the ground of his strong attachment to his native country, and especially cited the fact of his fitting out a vessel with Yankee lads from his Lancasterian School at Nantucket, to make master mariners of them, which could not be viewed by England with favor. So it may in truth be said that the Coffin School at Nantucket cost the Admiral an Earldom, and came near sacrificing his Baronetcy.

In 1790, when in command of the Alligator frigate, at the Nore, under sailing orders, the wind blowing strong, a man fell overboard. Coffin plunged in after him and saved his life; but in doing so sustained an injury from which he never fully recovered. It was regarded as a most heroic feat, and has once since been attempted by another descendant of Tristram, born at Nantucket, Lieut. Seth M. Ackley, of the U. S. Navy, who received therefor a commendatory letter from the Secretary of the Navy.

Isaac Coffin was commissioner of the Royal Navy in 1795, and was sent to Corsica; thence to Lisbon; thence to Mahon, in the Island of Minorca. Then he was placed in charge of the King's yard at Sheerness. He spent some time about the coast of Australia; and "Sir Isaac's Point" and "Coffin's Bay," as laid down on the English Coast Charts of Australia, are named in honor of him.

He married in 1811, Elizabeth, daughter of William Greenly, Esq., of Titley Court, Herefordshire; and, assuming the lady's name, became Sir Isaac Coffin Greenly. But the union was not a happy one, and they separated. She remained Lady Greenly and he dropped the Greenly. She was an exemplary lady, inclined to literary pursuits of a religious tendency which did not accord with his roilicking nature.

He at one time took to politics and was elected member of Parliament for Ilchester. Inclining to Liberalism, he consorted with the Whigs and became noted for his roug'0 humor and salt sayings.

Of his ready wit many stories are told—one will suffice. Once, on his way to Titley Court, stopping to bait at Chepstow, he was informed by the innkeeper that an American, a prisoner, confined in the castle hard by, claimed to be his relative, and prayed for an interview. Sir Isaac, curiously, acceded, went to the prison, and was introduced to "a gentleman of colour." Both surprised and amused, he was informed by Sambo that he was an American, a namesake, and must therefore be a relation, as no one would be likely to take his name for the fun of the thing. "Stop, my man, stop," interjected the Admiral, "let me ask you a question. Pray, how old may you be?" "Well," replied the other, "I should guess about thirty-five." "Oh! then," rejoined his interlocutor, turning away, "there is clearly a mistake here, you can't be one of my Coffins—none of my people ever turn black before they are forty." He nevertheless secured Sambo's release.

One day an American ship sailed into Portsmouth or Plymouth, England, before the war of 1812, when Sir Isaac had charge of the Naval fleet. An English officer was sent on board. The master having gone on shore, the mate being in charge did not receive the officer with the etiquette required on such occasions. The officer gave the first saluta-tion as he reached the deck, by saying "What kind of a d—d Yankee lubber has charge here, who don't know his duty to properly receive his majesty's officer?" The mate said not a word, but seizing his visitor by the collar and slack of his trousers threw him overboard, for his own crew to pick up. Soon after an armed boat came alongside to take the mate on board the flag ship, where he was arraigned before Sir Isaac, who soon became aware that the culprit was a kinsman, whose father he had been familiar with in boyhood. He tried to get the mate to acknowl-edge that he was ignorant of the laws and customs, that he might dismiss the case, with admonition, but the Yankee was obdurate: "He'd be d—d," he said, "if any man should insult him with impunity on his own deck and under the flag of his country." The offender was remanded to be regularly tried the next day. In the meantime the Admiral sent a messenger to privately inform the mate that a suitable apology would re-lieve him from any further trouble in the matter; but on the trial the same defiant manner was assumed. The Admiral drew out some ex-pression, however, which he accepted as satisfactory, and dismissed the offender with suitable admonitions.

Later in the day from the shore, the Admiral sent a message to the young man stating that, as his father was an old friend and relative, he would be happy to meet the son and enjoy a bottle of wine with him at the inn. But the young man replied that the Admiral might go to h—l with his wine. He'd see him d—d first before he'd drink with any d—d Englisher, especially one who would approve of an insult to an officer under his own flag upon his own deck.

The Admiral used to relate the above incident with much gusto, as he admired the spirit of independence exhibited by the Yankee mate.

Perhaps the most beneficial and truly philanthropic act of the Admi-ral was the founding of the Coffin School at Nantucket, a complete his-tory of which, written by George Howland Folger, Esq., a former pupil of the school, it is hoped will soon be presented to the public.

CAPT. SETH COFFIN, born at Nantucket, June 25, 1755, was a man of undaunted courage, as the following incident related to me by his great-granddaughter, Miss Emma V. Hallett, will abundantly exhibit. Capt. Coffin commanded a whaleship very young. In 1800, in the ship *Minerva*, off Brazil Banks, in the capture of a large sperm whale, Capt. Coffin's leg was crushed, and no one on board had knowledge of surgery suffi-cient to perform amputation except himself, and he had only witnessed one such a case under similar circumstances. So he called for an instru-ment used in cutting in whale's blubber, and then called his mate, and, bracing himself up on his couch, addressed his mate in this wise: "My leg has got to come off, or I shall die. I know how it should be done, and will show you how to do it. If you flinch one whit I'll send this in-strument through you. I am ready. Begin!" And the mate did begin, the captain instructing him how to take up each artery, and his leg was saved. When the last bandage was properly adjusted both men fainted.

JOSHUA COFFIN, ESQ., the historian of Newbury, was born at New-bury, in the old Coffin mansion, previously described, on the 12th of October, 1792, and died in the old home of his ancestors on the 24th of June, 1864, aged 73. He was a school teacher for many years, number-ing among his pupils John Greenleaf Whittier and Cornelius C. Felton, both of whom have spoken of their old teacher in high terms of praise; the poet owning a debt of gratitude in a noble poem. Mr. Coffin was much engaged in antiquarian pursuits and contributed much labor in that field. He published several works, and was by his neighbors sometimes called the "Walking Encyclopedia," there being scarcely any subject within the range of human knowledge that he had not examined, and his wonderfully retentive memory made him a storehouse of useful information.

LUCRETIA MOTT died at her residence near Philadelphia, on the evening of Nov. 11, 1880, at the advanced age of 87 years, 10 months and 8 days. She was born in Nantucket the third of January, A. D. 1793, in a house which stood on the spot now occupied by the residence of Capt. Obed Starbuck, on Fair street. Her father subsequently built the house now occupied by Judge T. C. Defriez, next south of her birth-place, in which her early childhood was passed. She was a direct descendant of the first Tristram Coffin on the paternal side, and of the first Peter Folger on the maternal side, her father bearing the name of Thomas Coffin and her mother that of Anna (Folger) Coffin.

In 1804, Lucretia then being only 11 years old, her parents removed to Boston. Here for about two years she attended the Boston schools with great advantage to herself. At the age of 13 she was sent to a Friends' Boarding School, in Dutchess County, New York, where she remained three years, during the last year employed as an assistant teacher, which shows how great her proficiency had been. Her parents, meantime, had removed to Philadelphia, where she subsequently joined them in 1809. Two years later, in 1811, at the age of 18, she was united in marriage with James Mott, of Philadelphia, who afterwards became a business partner of her father. Thus early settled in life the womanly duties of wife and mother devolved upon her, and were discharged with unerring fidelity, five out of six children born to her having arrived at maturity and lived to the credit of their mother's excellent example.

She was an approved minister of the Society of Friends, and in 1827, took sides with Elias Hicks, and was thereafter known as a Hicksite.

Her active mind, directed and developed by the peculiar teachings of her religious sect, took a wider range than had previously been customary with women, and she gave of her best offerings to the world. In all the great moral reforms she took an active part, manifesting a great interest in the advancement of the working classes, frequently attending their meetings, and adding her testimony to the righteousness of their cause. She was unquestionably the most gifted woman of her time, and used her gifts with consummate wisdom. As a spiritual, moral and intellectual force of the nineteenth century she had no superior the world over. Her power of speech was almost divine; her "words were gold coined in the mint of a royal mind;" whatever her hand touched, it blessed; whatever her warm sympathy became attached to, grew in stature and comeliness. She was the bright morning star of intellectual freedom in America, and she helped break the chains which bound a race in physical slavery. But for the fact that her death was to have been expected, the announcement would have spread a gloom throughout the bounds of civilization. The idol of to-day may crowd the hero of yesterday from the speech of mankind; but the life of Lucretia Mott has left an influence upon the world which time cannot destroy or efface; and, so long as there is left a chord in the heart of humanity which beats responsively to the truth and purity of her life, so long will there be pilgrims journeying to her tomb to drop thereon in mingled profusion white flowers and tears.

PROF. JAMES HENRY COFFIN, LL. D., was born at Williamsburg, near Northampton, Mass., Sept. 6, 1806, and was sixty-six years and five months old at the time of his death. Being left a poor orphan, he went to live with his uncle, the Rev. Moses Hallock, under whose care he was educated. He graduated at Amherst College in 1828. After leaving college he engaged in teaching in Massachusetts, entering upon a profession in which he continued until the day of his death. He established one of the first manual labor schools in the country, at Greenfield, Mass., which was known as the Fellenberg Academy. Leaving Greenfield in 1837, he went to Ogdensburg, N. Y., to take charge of a school there. Here he remained till 1839. His scientific life dates from this time. Here he became interested in Meteorology. In 1839 he left Ogdensburg to become a tutor in Williams College, where he remained five years. Here he published a work on the mode of calculating solar and lunar eclipses, which was extensively used. During the same period he devised the erection and superintended the building of the Greylock Observatory on Saddle Mountain. In this observatory he placed the first combined, self-registering instrument to determine the direction, velocity and moisture of winds, ever constructed. An improved instrument for the same purpose he recently presented to the Observatory at Cordova, Buenos Ayres. Leaving Williams College in 1843, he spent three years in teaching at Norwalk, Conn. In 1844 an acquaintanceship began, which continued up to the time of the rebellion, between the Professor and Capt. M. F. Maury, U. S. N. Capt. Maury is well known for his investigations into the subject of oceanic currents and winds. In 1846 Prof. Coffin accepted the position of Professor of Mathematics in Lafayette College, and for twenty-seven years his life has been spent in Easton. As Professor of Mathematics at Lafayette, Dr. Coffin won much celebrity, but his name will, perhaps, be more widely known throughout the country as a contributor to the reports of the Smithsonian Institution, and for his investigations on the subject of winds and atmospheric changes. In this field he was a pioneer. Twenty-two years ago the Smithsonian Institution published a large quarto volume of Prof. Coffin's, on the Winds of the Northern Hemisphere. For some years he was engaged on another work, which at the time of his death was nearly ready for publication. This volume was a treatise on the "Winds of the Globe." Issued by Smithsonian Institution, 1876—pages 781 ; 26 plates, the largest numerical tables ever issued from the American press. Among his more important mathematical works are a "Treatise on Solar and Lunar Eclipses," a work on the "Meteoric Fire-ball of July, 1860," "Astronomical Tables," "Conic Sections," and "Analytical Geometry."

The merits and learning of Dr. Coffin were not unrecognized. He was one of the first elected members of the National Academy of Science, and was a prominent member of the American Association for the Advancement of Science, at whose meetings he frequently read papers on meteorological subjects. At the time of his death, on the sixth of February, 1873, he was an elder in the Brainerd Church. He united with the church at an early age, and lived a sincere and devout christian.

CAPT. REUBEN COFFIN, of Athens, N. Y., was in command of steamer *Seth Low*, during the war of the Rebellion, chartered to tow from New

York to James River the *Monitor*, with orders to proceed with all possible dispatch. When running down the coast with the *Monitor* in tow, a heavy fog set in with a heavy sea. The United States officers on board in command of the *Monitor* wanted Captain Coffin, of the *Low*, to cast anchor, as the lead showed they were shoaling their water and might get ashore. Captain Coffin told the officers he would run off shore and that would give more water, that his orders were to proceed with all possible dispatch, and he was not going to stop unless compelled to, and kept on his course, and reached his destination during the night previous to the famous fight between the *Monitor* and *Merrimack*. Never had any arrival proved more fortunate. The *Monitor* saved the balance of the United States fleet not already destroyed. This act of Captain Coffin in keeping on his course against the protests of the United States officers saved many valuable lives, and the government millions of money.

THE COFFIN COAT OF ARMS.

Heraldry has a language all its own, the significance of which none but careful students who have made it a specialty will pretend to absolute accuracy in its exposition. Briefly stated, it is the science of conventional distinctions impressed on shields or banners, and is both national and personal. The latter treats of bearings belonging to individuals either in their own or hereditary right. The Coffins have always claimed Coat Armour in hereditary right. That branch descended from Nathaniel Coffin, father of Admiral Sir Isaac, inherit the right through the Admiral's grant, and are unquestionably entitled to wear his Coat of Arms, but this differs essentially in its emblazonment from the more ancient ones.

Authorities upon English heraldry give, as belonging to the Coffins of Devonshire, a description which, in its combination, is unlike any other family bearings, and consists of Bezants and Cross-Crosslets. While they differ as to order of arrangement and combination, the number of Bezants is never less than three nor more than four, and the Cross-Crosslets vary from five upward to a semee which is an indefinite convenient number.

The Bezants are a roundle representing the ancient gold coin of Byzantium, current in England from the tenth century to the time of Edward III., and was probably introduced into coat armour by the crusaders. The white roundle exhibited upon Admiral Sir Isaac's Arms, is of silver, and is usually called a plate, although there were silver bezants used as coin. The Cross-Crosslets are Crosses crossed on each arm.

The Crests and Mottoes are of quite modern origin.

CLAN COFFIN.

Memorial  Reunion.

GREAT GATHERING OF THE

𝕯𝖊𝖘𝖈𝖊𝖓𝖉𝖆𝖓𝖙𝖘 𝖔𝖋 𝕿𝖗𝖎𝖘𝖙𝖗𝖆𝖒 𝕮𝖔𝖋𝖋𝖎𝖓,

ON THE ISLAND OF NANTUCKET,

August 16th, 17th and 18th, 1881.

The Executive Committee of the Tristram Coffin Reunion Association having received numerous responses from members of the family in all parts of the country, and having made important progress in the arrangements for the bi-centennial, referred to in their previous circular of invitation, are now enabled to announce that the Grand Reunion will be held on the Island of Nantucket, the exercises to continue three days, commencing on Tuesday, the 16th day of August, 1881. The programme, as now definitely arranged, will include the following:

FIRST DAY.—On August 16, a Grand Clambake, to come off near the site of Tristram Coffin's dwelling house of two centuries ago. On this occasion an oration will be made by Tristram Coffin, Esq., of Poughkeepsie, N. Y., followed by the usual feast of reason and flow of soul incident to such occasions, a mammoth tent being erected for the purpose.

SECOND DAY.—On August 17, the memorial exercises with procession and corner-stone ceremonies. Charles Carleton Coffin, Esq., of Boston, will pronounce the oration, and Robert Barry Coffin, Esq., of New York, will probably act as the poet of the occasion.

THIRD DAY.—On August 18, a breakfast will come off under the mammoth tent, with appropriate incidentals. Prof. Selden J. Coffin, of Lafayette College, Pennsylvania, will deliver the oration on this occasion. A Grand Ball at night will close the exercises.

On all of the days other literary and musical exercises appropriate to the times and places may be anticipated, and all the descendants of the illustrious ancestor are invited to contribute something in speech or song to make the celebration emphatically a family reunion.

At a meeting of the Executive Committee held in August last, it was voted to erect two bronze statues representing the patriarch Tristram Coffin and Dionis Coffin, his wife, upon a broad pedestal, at an estimated expense of from eight to ten thousand dollars. In view of the spirit already displayed in the matter, it is hoped and believed that the many descendants of those who are to be thus honored will be prompt in responding to the call, and will contribute liberally to make up the desired amount with the least possible delay. It is earnestly desired that, in response to this circular, all members of the Coffin family who intend to be present at the Reunion shall signify such intention in advance, and, if possible, at an early date, as the plans of the Committee will be much facilitated by their so doing.

Those wishing to contribute to the Memorial Fund for the erection of the statues are earnestly requested to signify in writing the sums, larger or smaller, which they will be ready to contribute. It is also important that all persons responding by letter to this call should write their full names, giving both christian and surname, and also middle name if they may have one. If possible, they may also state the name of parents and grandparents, showing to what line of the Coffin family they belong, as such information may be interesting and valuable.

A collection of articles used by members of the family in olden time will be gathered together for exhibition during the week of festivities.

The Committee have in contemplation the publication of a Life of Tristram Coffin, the founder of the family line in America, and from whom all persons by the name of Coffin in this country are descended, together with reminiscences of some of his most illustrious descendants. An outline of the family history from the earliest reliable data will also be given, illustrated with the different Coats of Arms, and other interesting views. The profits to go toward defraying the expenses of the celebration.

Photograph copies of eight different oil paintings of some of the descendants of the first Richard Coffin, which now adorn the walls of Portledge, near Bideford, Devon County, England, and who flourished in the fifteenth and sixteenth centuries, it is hoped will be offered for sale in aid of the celebration fund.

It is also expected that medals will be struck commemorative of the two-hundredth anniversary of the death of the American ancestor, appropriately inscribed, that all who attend the Reunion may carry away with them a fitting memento of the celebration, the proceeds to be applied to the celebration fund.

All correspondence should be addressed to the Secretary and Treasurer, Allen Coffin, Nantucket, Mass.

Articles of Association.

This association shall be known as THE TRISTRAM COFFIN REUNION ASSOCIATION.

The object shall be the commemoration of the two-hundredth anniversary of the death of Tristram Coffin (the first of the race who settled in America), October 2, 1881.

Its officers shall consist of a President, seven Vice-Presidents, a Secretary and Treasurer, and an Executive Committee of thirty, the Vice-Presidents and Executive Board being delegated with power to increase their numbers at any time.

Any person who is a descendant or married to a descendant of Tristram Coffin may become a member of this association by proving the same and paying to the Treasurer an admission fee of fifty cents.

Officers.

President,

CHARLES G. COFFIN, ESQ., of Nantucket.

Vice-Presidents,

Capt. OLIVER C. COFFIN,   Nantucket, Mass.
WILLIAM C. FOLGER, Esq.   "   "
JAMES B. COFFIN,   "   "
Mrs. ELIZA BARNEY,   "   "
Miss ANNA GARDNER,   "   "
Rev. HERBERT W. COFFIN, Plymouth, Mass.
Miss ANNA L. COFFIN, Newburyport, Mass.
CHARLES CARLETON COFFIN, Esq., Boston, Mass.
WILLIAM E. COFFIN, Esq.,   "   "
EDWARD P. COFFIN, Northfield, Me.

Secretary and Treasurer,

ALLEN COFFIN, Nantucket, Mass.

Executive Committee.

ALLEN COFFIN, Esq.,   Nantucket, Mass.
WILLIAM H. MACY, Esq.,   "   "
Judge THADDEUS C. DEFRIEZ,   "   "
Mrs. ELIZABETH G. M. BARNEY,   "   "
Mrs. ANNE MITCHELL MACY,   "   "
Rev. HOWARD A. HANAFORD,   "   "
JOHN A. COFFIN,   "   "
ARTHUR H. GARDNER,   "   "
ROLAND B. HUSSEY,   "   "
ALEXANDER MACY,   "   "
SAMUEL F. COFFIN,   "   "
Miss AMELIA M. COFFIN,   "   "
Miss STELLA L. CHASE,   "   "
Mrs. CHARLOTTE A. JOY,   "   "
Mrs. HARRIET PEIRCE,   "   "
MOSES JOY, Jr.,   "   "
CHARLES F. BROWN, San Francisco, Cal.
WILLIAM M. BUNKER,   "   "
WILLIAM E. COFFIN, Richmond, Ind.
ALEXANDER STARBUCK, Waltham, Mass.
Prof. MARIA MITCHELL, Vassar College, Poughkeepsie, N. Y.
HENRY W. COFFIN, New York, N. Y.
Rev. PHEBE A. HANAFORD, Jersey City, N. J.
Rev. FERDINAND C. EWER, D. D., New York, N. Y.
Judge OWEN TRISTRAM COFFIN, Peekskill, N. Y.
Chief Justice CHARLES J. FOLGER, Albany, N. Y.
TRISTRAM COFFIN, Esq., Poughkeepsie, N. Y.
ROLAND F. COFFIN, Esq., Brooklyn, N. Y.
Mrs. MARY COFFIN JOHNSON, Brooklyn, N. Y.
Miss CHARLOTTE E. COFFIN, Brooklyn, N. Y.
Mrs. REBECCA CLAPP MORSE, Hartford, Conn.
Miss EMMA V. HALLETT,   "   "
Mrs. MARIA L. OWEN, Springfield, Mass.
Prof. SELDEN J. COFFIN, Lafayette College, Easton, Pa.
CHARLES COFFIN, Esq., Walnut Ridge, Ark.
GEORGE M. COFFIN, Honolulu, Sandwich Islands.
SAMUEL L. COFFIN, College of Pharmacy, Chicago, Ill.
EDWARD M. COFFIN, Esq., Ord, Nebraska.
EDWARD W. COFFIN, Esq., Camden, N. J.
CHARLES E. COFFIN, Cincinnati, O.
HECTOR COFFIN, Knoxville, Tenn.
D. W. COFFIN, Indianapolis, Ind.
DON CARLOS TUFTS, Salt Lake City, Utah.

Inquirer and Mirror Press.

Tristram Coffin Reunion Association.

The Tristram Coffin Reunion Association, at its late meetings in Nantucket, Mass., continuing from the 15th to the 18th days of August, 1881, was enabled to do considerable business of a most important character, and to organize committees for facilitating the future operations of the Association. Having no corporate existence under the laws of Massachusetts, it was voted to perpetuate the Association under its present organization and officers. The President and Secretary and Treasurer were constituted a committee to secure an act of incorporation, adapted to the objects of the Association.

The subject of erecting a monument called forth most enthusiastic expression in its favor, and varied opinions as to what kind it should be. No definite conclusion was arrived at, however, and it will remain for subsequent action. It is known that very many members present did not subscribe to the monument fund because no plan or model of the same had been submitted or agreed upon. Notwithstanding the indefinite condition of the monument project, something over eleven hundred dollars have been subscribed for that purpose, and a portion of the same paid in, as will appear in the financial statement herewith presented.

A committee on the history and genealogy of the Coffin family was appointed, consisting of George Howland Folger, Esq., and John Coffin Jones Brown, Esq., of Boston, Mass.; Alexander Starbuck, of Waltham, Mass.; Zebulon Butler Coffin, of Cincinnati, O.; and William Edward Coffin, of Richmond, Ind. Prof. Selden J. Coffin, of Easton, Pa., and Rev. Phebe A. Hanaford, of Jersey City, N. J., were subsequently added to the committee by vote of the Association. The committee also have power to add to their number if they desire. It was voted that, if any balance in the general fund be found remaining after all the expenses of the Reunion had been paid, it should be applied to the use of the committee on history and genealogy.

Forty States and Territories, including foreign nationalities, are now represented by active members.

For the general purposes of the Association for the ensuing year an assessment of fifty cents per capita was voted. As it is not to be expected that members not present can know of this assessment, and perhaps many who were present may have forgotten the vote, the attention of all members is herein respectfully called to the same.

ALLEN COFFIN, *Secretary and Treasurer.*

Financial.

The committee appointed to audit the accounts of Mr. Allen Coffin, Secretary and Treasurer of the Tristram Coffin Reunion Association, respectfully report that they have examined the said accounts, and find the proper vouchers for the principal charges. In consequence of the overwhelming amount of business that devolved upon the Secretary and Treasurer during the exercises, and the large amount of money received at that time, he was unable to keep such an account in detail as he otherwise would have done, and is obliged to present his account of receipts and expenses as herewith appended:

Tristram Coffin Reunion Association in account with Allen Coffin, Secretary and Treasurer.

1881. Dr.		1881. Cr.	
Sept. 1. For cash paid as follows, viz:		Sept. 1. By cash received, viz:	
A. F. Copeland, Banquet and Clambake,	$1103.00	598 membership fees, at 50 cents each,	$299.00
Brass Band,	201.00	Mrs. Eliza Nevins, donation,	100.00
Expenses, do.,	25.00	Mr. Andrew G. Coffin, donation,	25.00
C. E. Wiggin, crockery,	518.11	Sales o' Crockery,	628.00
1500 copies Life of Tristram Coffin,	180.00	From sales of pictures of Tristram Coffin, as taken from the Admiral medal, donated by George H. Folger, of Boston; pictures of the old Coffin homestead at Newbury, donated by William E. Coffin, of Richmond, Ind.; Hector Coffin Coat of Arms, donated by Charles H. Coffin, of New Bedford, and the Life of Tristram Coffyn, prepared by the Secretary,	265.90
Postages and Envelopes,	15.84		
Blank book,	.95		
Carriages,	23.00		
Carting,	9.05		
Coats of arms and photographs,	65.25		
Printing,	86.59		
Ball Expenses,	35.70		
Ribbon and Cotton Cloth,	41.11		
Cots,	50.00		
Hall Rents,	49.00		
Police,	10.85	Sales of Ball Tickets,	121.00
Express and Freight,	13.19	From all other sources, including sales of tickets to Clambake, Concert and Banquet,	1157.88
Town Crier,	2.10		
Expenses to Boston, 4 trips,	40.00		
Carpenters' work,	8.88		
Balloons,	4.00		
Cleaning Methodist Church,	5.00		
Sept. 1. Balance Cash in Treasurer's hands,	116.53		
	$2599.78		$2599.78

Subscriptions to Monument Fund.

1881.	
Jan. 17, Cyrus Woodman, Cambridge, Mass., $10 for each of the statues,	$20.00
Jan. 24, Tristram Coffin, Poughkeepsie, N. Y.,	25.00
Feb. 15, Owen Tristram Coffin, Peekskill, N. Y.,	25.00
Mch. 4, Edward Winslow Coffin, Camden, N. J.,	10.00
May 31, James Gardner Coffin, Pittsburgh, Pa.,	15.00
July 22, Admiral John Townsend Coffin, R. N., England,	14.10
Aug. 15, Charles Coffin, Dutchess Co., N. Y.,	25.00
" " George W. Coffin, California,	25.00
" " William H. Coffin, New York City,	25.00
" " R. G. Coffin, Dutchess Co., N. Y.,	25.00
	$209.10

Amount brought forward,		$520.40
Aug. 16, Tristram Coffin, Poughkeepsie, N. Y., (2d subscription),		25.00
" " William M. Bunker, San Francisco,		4.50
" " Elmira P. Tufts, Salt Lake City, Utah,		4.50
" " Don Carlos Tufts, " " " "		25.00
" " Charles F. Brown, San Francisco, Cal.,		25.00
" 18, Selden J. Coffin, Easton, Pa.,		25.00
" " Allen Coffin, Nantucket, Mass.,		25.00
" " Zebulon B. Coffin, Cincinnati, O.,		25.00
" " Uriah H. Coffin, Boston, Mass.,		25.00
" " Rev. Phebe A. Hanaford, Jersey City, N. J.,		25.00
" " Edmund Coffin, New York City,		25.00
" " Andrew G. Coffin, " " "		25.00
" " I. Sherwood Coffin, " " "		25.00
" " D. W. Coffin, Indianapolis, Ind.,		50.00
" " Mrs. Charlotte C. Pearson, Nantucket, Mass.,		25.00
" " Mrs. Sarah F. C. Baxter, Rutland, Vt.,		25.00
(and $25 a year until monument is completed.)		
" " Mrs. Eliza Barney, Nantucket, Mass.,		25.00
" " Benjamin F. Coffin, " "		25.00
" " Mrs. Anna B. Kelley, Boston, "		25.00
" " Mrs. Eliza S. Nevins, Brighton, "		100.00
" " David Nevins, " "		100.00
" " Henry Coffin Nevins, " "		100.00
" " Amelia French Milborn,		10.00
" " Mrs. John H. Inman, New York, N. Y.,		100.00
" " Mrs. James W. Harle, Atlanta, Ga.,		25.00
Sept. 1, Miss Emma V. Hallett, from sales of Coats of Arms,		20.00
		$1120.40

Cash in the Treasurer's hands belonging to the general account,	116.53
Cash in the Treasurer's hands collected from subscriptions to the Monument Fund,	290.40
Total amount in Treasurer's hands,	$406.93

The Treasurer has also on hand property unsold, belonging to the Association, as follows, viz:

94 Plates. Cost value,	$47.00
133 Cups and Saucers,	66.50
232 Hector Coffin Coat of Arms,	4.64
15 Photographs of Tristram Coffin,	3.75
1284 copies, unbound, Life of Tristram Coffyn,	154.08
27 " bound, " " "	12.69
	$288.66

Also, a lot of valuable mineral specimens, the gift of Mrs. Elmira P. Tufts, of Salt Lake City, Utah.

Amount of outstanding bills not presented, estimated at $60.

OLIVER C. COFFIN,
ANDREW WHITNEY,   } *Auditing Committee.*
THADDEUS C. DEFRIEZ,

Nantucket, Sept. 1, 1881.

Comments:

It is evidently carefully and thoroughly prepared, and contains much that is of great interest, not only to the Coffin family, but to all interested in historical and biographical matters.—*New Bedford Standard.*

Besides an interesting sketch of the life of the founder of the Coffin family in America, contains reminiscences and anecdotes of some of his numerous descendants, and historical information concerning the ancient families of the name.—*New Bedford Mercury.*

It is evidently the result of laborious research, and will commend itself not only to the numerous branches of the Coffin family, but to others interested in the history of the early settlement of Nantucket.— *Whalemen's Shipping List.*

The author appears to have done his work thoroughly, and to have exhausted the subject, always substantiating his statements by documentary evidence, whenever such could be obtained.—*Nantucket Inquirer and Mirror.*

Proves the entire story of Thomas Macy's flight in an open boat, which furnished the theme for Whittier's beautiful poem, "The Exiles," to have been a myth. Every islander and every person claiming Coffin descent should possess themselves of a copy.—*Nantucket Journal.*

The tribe of Coffin is indebted to you for work well done in the outline of the history of the family.—*John Coffin Jones Brown.*

With your pamphlet pages of "Life of Tristram Coffyn" I am delighted. You have dug deep.—*Prof. Selden J. Coffin, Lafayette College, Pa.*

I enjoyed the Life of our Old Ancestor, which you sent me, very much; and, for myself, am under great obligations to you for the time you must have spent in looking up the old records.— *William E. Coffin, of Boston.*

    *   *   * For the great industry in procuring information not before published in relation to the family, and for giving the first true history within my knowledge in relation to the settlement of Nantucket, its founders and their motives.—*George Howland Folger, of Cambridge.*